# Wild IRISH

## BROOKE O'BRIEN

# Dedication

To anyone who has supported me on this journey,
thank you. This one is for you!

BROOKE O'BRIEN

# AUSTEN

I'll never forget how scared I was sitting in the back of a police car.

It's one of those memories that's hard to wipe away from your mind. It was after three in the morning when the cops showed up at our apartment. Without explanation, they instructed me to come with them because they were taking my mom to jail.

It wasn't the first time she'd been arrested, and sadly, I knew it wouldn't be the last. What I didn't know at the time, while tears streaked down my face, was this time would be different.

She wouldn't be coming home for at least five years.

The days after I arrived at Haven Brook were the hardest of my life. Every day I waited in the hopes my dad, or someone in my family, would show up to take me away. I'd have the home I desperately wanted to have growing up.

Every day I went to bed disappointed and heartbroken.

I didn't have a lot of friends, especially at Haven Brook. That's what first drew me to Ryder. He was quiet, kept to himself. I've only ever heard him talk when he was being spoken to, and even then, he didn't have much to say. He'd give clipped, one- or two-word responses. He blew most people off, never giving them the time of day.

I've heard the whispers about him. He's one of the longest residents at Haven Brook. I guess watching the other kids come and go, their parents coming back to get them, stuck with him over time.

I always wondered what it was about him and his past that made him so closed off.

So, when I woke up in the middle of the night to find him standing over me, I immediately had alarm bells going off in my head.

"Are you okay?" he whispers.

"What the hell are you doing in here, Ryder?" I push myself up in my bed, glancing around the bedroom.

There are four bedrooms in total, and each one has four beds a piece. Two rooms for the girls and two for the boys. I claimed one of the spots in the far back corner. The bed is pushed back into a small nook built into the wall. Something about it felt safe, cozy.

Ryder is in the boy's room across the hall from me.

"I was up getting a glass of water, and I heard you crying."

I reach my hand up, dabbing it along my cheek, finding it damp from my tears. I brush my fingers through my hair before pulling the blanket up under my chin, staring up at his bright blue eyes. Even in the darkness, I can still see them sparkling like crystals. They remind me of what I'd imagine the ocean looks like.

The stark contrast between his dark hair, longer on top, to the color of his eyes is something that's caught the attention of the other girls at Haven Brook. If he noticed, he didn't seem to care.

He clears his throat, and I snap out of it. I shake my head, gazing down at my blanket, trying to remember what he had said.

*Oh, right, the dream.*

I've been having the same dream over and over for the past three nights. It is less of a dream and more like a flashback. We were living in our apartment on the other side of town. It wasn't much, but it was the best my mom could find with low-income housing.

I got used to waking up in the middle of the night from the sounds of fighting and emergency sirens going off. Our neighbors next door had a tendency of getting into it and airing their dirty laundry for the rest of the complex to hear. A few times I was woken up by gunshots going off. Those were the nights I didn't sleep at all.

Somehow, I got so used to the sounds around me that I couldn't help but fear the nights when it was quiet too. That's how the night I've been dreaming of started out. Something about the silence around me filled me with unease.

I always knew when my mom came home by the sound of our screen door slamming shut. It was my way of knowing she made it home safe that night.

I remember pushing the blanket off me, swinging my legs over the side, and climbing out of bed. The floorboards creaked under my footsteps, peeking my head out of my room and down the hall.

I was hit with the strong smell of burnt plastic. It still causes my stomach to roll at the memory. I lifted my shirt to cover my face as I tiptoed down the hallway.

I can still see everything so clearly in my mind. The blinds were closed; only the TV and the light above the stove were on, making it hard to see. I almost missed her when I did my first sweep. A niggling thought in the back of my mind forced me to check again, wanting to make sure my mom was okay.

It was everything after that moment that felt like a whirlwind. I collapsed to the floor next to my mom when I found the used syringe on the floor nearby. She was face down in a pool of her own vomit.

"Are you sure you're okay?" Ryder asks. I shake my head again, snapping myself out of the memory. His brows furrow in concern.

"I'm good." I nod, staring at the wildflowers printed on the comforter. I run my fingers over the silk edges, helping calm the thoughts running through my mind.

"You didn't sound okay when I walked in here."

This is the most I've ever heard him speak. To know he's never shown interest in anyone, yet, wanted to come in here to make sure I'm okay, made heat radiate through my body.

"Yeah, it's just a bad dream," I mutter, scrubbing my hands over my face. "I'll be okay. I always am."

He glances around the room. I expect him to turn and head back to his before he peers down at me.

"Would it make you feel better if I stayed in here with you? I can grab a blanket and a pillow and lie here on the floor."

My stomach flutters. All those uncertain nights of going to sleep alone, wondering if or when my mom would come home, flash through my mind.

"Sure," I murmur. "If you don't mind sleeping on the floor. I would appreciate it."

He disappears out of the room without a word and returns a minute later with his comforter and pillow under his arm. I feel bad for making him sleep on the floor when he tosses his pillow next to my nightstand and kneels on the ground beside me.

"Are you sure you want to sleep down there? It doesn't look the least bit comfortable."

"Where else am I going to sleep? I can't exactly lie up there with you."

I picture him crawling into bed next to me when he says it. It's not that I wouldn't let him or don't want him to, which is crazy to say given I barely know him. I'm more afraid of what sort of trouble we'd get into if anyone woke up and caught us.

They'd get the wrong idea, and Lord knows how it would get spun, landing us in a bigger mess.

I peer over the bed at him, ready to tell him I'm okay with it if he is, when he shakes his head.

"I was kidding," he whispers. "Go to sleep, Austen. I'll be right here if you need anything."

I nod, releasing a heavy sigh before collapsing on my pillow. I stare up at the neon stars stuck to the ceiling. We sit in silence for a few minutes before I roll over again, tilting my head over the side of the bed.

"You're staring," he says with his eyes closed. "It's weird."

"I'm not staring. I was just going to say thank you," I fire back, my chest tightening.

He doesn't move or say anything. I drag my bottom lip through my teeth before falling back onto my pillow, forcing my eyes closed.

Ryder is gone when I wake up. I'm not surprised. I'm sure he snuck back to his room before everyone woke up.

I spot him sitting at one of the picnic tables in the backyard after school. He has a notebook spread open in front of him. His tall frame is bent over, focused on his drawing.

"Hey, how was school?" I ask, moving my leg over the bench seat as he slams his notebook shut.

His eyes shoot over to mine, watching as I sit down across from him. I try to flash him a warm smile, hoping to ease whatever tension is building between us. Any kindness I saw the night before is gone, replaced with a cold look I recognize as the Ryder I knew every day before.

He doesn't bother to respond. Not unless you consider the glare he flashes my way a response.

"Is everything okay?"

"I'm just trying to figure out why you're talking to me."

"Excuse me?" I fire back.

"You're excused," he mutters coldly, dismissing me from the conversation.

I scoff, standing back up and adjust my backpack over my shoulder.

"What the hell is your problem?"

He shrugs. "Listen, just because I do you a favor, doesn't make us friends."

I smirk, my brows shooting up in surprise. This kid honestly thinks me, or anyone else around here, would consider him a friend?

"You've gotta be kidding me. You did me a favor?" I laugh. "Why don't you do yourself a favor? Get over yourself and fuck off."

He remains stoic, staring at me. He blinks slowly, waiting for me to leave. The beautiful eyes I saw the night before turn to ice, fitting for the cold person sitting in front of me.

"What would make you think I'd want to be friends with you anyway? Do you even have any?"

His face is hard, unreadable. It only seems to grind on my nerves more. He reaches for his books, shoving them into his bag.

He's wearing a worn pair of denim jeans and a graphic T-shirt with "loser" plastered in large block letters.

I move past him, not bothering to waste another second on him or this conversation. He reaches for my hand, stopping me in my tracks. He takes a step toward me, pinning me against the edge of the table.

His brows furrow, and his jaw is set, reminding me of the way an animal stalks their prey.

He quirks his brow, waiting for me to push him away. He's taunting me, hoping I'll crack right before him.

"You really are an asshole, you know that?" I mutter.

He smirks again. This time when he leans in close, he brushes his nose along my jaw up toward my ear, his breath feathering over my skin.

"If you listen closely, you can hear the sound of me not giving a fuck."

He reaches around, grabbing his bag and stalks away from me.

I sag against the edge of the table and cross my arms.

As much as I want to hate him, I hate myself more for how bad I want him.

# AUSTEN
## *Four Years Later*

*"Damn, I wish I was there with you gorgeous."*

*"Goddamn, you're beautiful."*

*"Lord, the things I'd do to you."*

I sigh, scrolling through the comments on my picture from last night. I click "like" on each one before locking my phone and shove it into my pocket.

Sometimes I feel like I'm living a double life, but I guess if I think about it, I am.

To the internet, I'm Violet Grace. To the rest of the world, I'm Austen Fox.

I drag my hand over my face and release a sigh of relief, staring at the empty dorm room. It's only me and my two suitcases now, but it's all I need.

I've been waiting for this day for what feels like forever. I busted my ass in school and took on a new job just so I can leave the hellhole of my hometown and get into Eastwood University.

I did it. I'm finally here.

I never thought I'd be sharing intimate photos or videos online as a way of making money, but between going to school full-time and my internship, I didn't see any other way.

I push myself to my feet and walk over to the mirror hanging on the wall. I smile at my reflection, raking a hand through my long dark brown hair matching my eyes. I take in the cropped tank top and black denim shorts with studs along the pocket.

I roll my shoulders back, shaking out my hair to give it some life, and reach into my pocket for my phone. I lift my shirt up in the mirror, and the camera clicks, snapping a few pictures in various poses.

I always try to be cautious of my surroundings, not wanting to give any clues as to who or where I am. Although, I've come to find the ones in the riskiest places earn the best tips.

"Jesus, Aimee!" I hear, followed by a heavy grunt. "How many fuckin' suitcases do you need?"

I frantically spin on my heels, dropping my phone on the floor in the process.

"Austen?"

I release an audible gasp when my eyes fall on him. What the hell is Ryder O'Rourke doing standing in my dorm?

His eyes do a full sweep of my body, landing on my chest. His lip quirks in a smile before continuing their slow pursual, ending with his gaze locking on mine. His brows shoot up, and it's apparent he didn't realize who he was gawking at until his eyes met mine.

"Excuse you," I mutter. "Do you always waltz through people's doors unannounced?"

He drags two large suitcases into the room, heaving one of them onto Aimee's bed, before turning his attention back on me.

"I didn't think anyone was here." He glares.

He's changed over the years, yet so much of him reminds me of the boy I knew back at Haven Brook.

He stands tall, his broad shoulders filling the doorway. He carries himself with confidence, his bright blue eyes framing his handsome square face. He's wearing a black T-shirt with the words "fuck your feelings" printed across the front. His hair is buzzed to his scalp, and I briefly wonder what it would feel like against my skin.

There's a commotion in the hallway, and he points his

finger at my chest.

I look down, turning to check myself out in the mirror. Heat blazes over my cheeks when I notice my bra tucked into my shirt, the two tangled together during my desperate attempt to cover myself up.

I press my lips together, staring at Ryder in the mirror wearing a smirk on his face. I blink my wide eyes at him as if telling him to turn the hell around. He shakes his head and focuses on moving the other suitcase near the foot of Aimee's bed.

"What are you doing here anyway?" he quips when I turn back around.

"What am I doing here?" I repeat, wondering the same thing. "I live here. This is my dorm."

"You ..." he draws out. "You're staying here with Aimee?"

I can't believe this is even possible. I haven't seen Ryder since I left Haven Brook. I was there for a week before my mom was released on bond and finally got me out of there.

Ryder was still there, still being an asshole every day until the day I left. He never came to my room again and we never spoke about that night either.

I always wondered why he cared enough to comfort me, only to turn around and treat me like he didn't give a shit the next.

"Are you going to move your ass, Ryder?" A woman huffs. Judging by the sass in her tone, I'm going to throw out a guess it is Aimee. I can picture her standing behind him, arms crossed in frustration.

Ryder stands in the doorway, blocking her from coming through.

I exchanged a few texts with Aimee when we found out we'd be rooming together, but we haven't spoken since.

She comes barreling through the door a moment later, pushing Ryder out of the way as she does. Her bright smile is infectious, her blonde hair bouncing in a ponytail behind her as she rushes toward me, wrapping her arms around me in a hug.

Ryder watches me stand frozen in place, using his fist to cover his laugh. I warm up to her, though, patting my hand along her back to return her greeting. It is safe to say I'm not used to the affection like she is.

"It's so good to finally meet you." She grins. She pulls back, glancing from me and back to Ryder.

"You, too." I smile. "Is this your boyfriend?"

Aimee wags her brows, sauntering over to Ryder, wrapping her arm around his waist. He pushes her away, hollering "Darren" before another man comes up to stand behind him.

My eyes glance between the three of them, trying to figure out their dynamic.

"Or is this one of those throuples? I've always wondered how they work. I mean, whatever you're into is cool with me."

"A what?" Ryder's eyes bulge, pushing away from the two of them.

Darren's gaze turns dark, and Aimee throws her head back in a fit of giggles. I have no idea what's up with either of them, but I'm glad Aimee can at least laugh it off.

"Not at all." She presses her hand against her stomach, trying to catch her breath. "Darren is my boyfriend."

She gestures toward the broody man, who finally pushes his way into the room practically tossing the last suitcase next to the others. Between him and Ryder, it's safe to say they both have their panties in a wad.

What would someone as sweet and outgoing as Aimee want with the two of them?

"Austen, I think the two of us are going to get along just fine." Aimee smiles, her heels clicking on the floor as she saunters over and collapses on her bed.

"Wait," Aimee asks, pushing herself up onto her elbows. "What happened between the two of you when we got here? I heard him call you Austen. Do you know each other?"

My head snaps over to Ryder, not sure how I should answer the question.

"I bumped into her with the door when I walked in. I didn't know she was on the other side. I only know her name because you mentioned it when we were driving over here."

Her eyes narrow. She looks between the two of us, trying to gauge if he's telling the truth. She gives us a slow nod, not quite sure if she believes him.

"I need to go back out to the car and grab a couple bags. Darren, will you help me? We can leave our two new *friends* here to get their story straight."

She moves to stand, flashing me a wink for my eyes only when she walks past. She drags her long pink fingernail along Ryder's chest when she passes him, spinning around to face us as she reaches for the doorknob.

"Have fun." She wags her brows, and Darren shakes his head before she closes the door behind them.

I look back at Ryder, confused as to what happened and how I managed to end up standing here alone with him after all these years. It all happened so quickly, I could barely catch up.

He stalks toward the door, appearing to leave when he reaches for the door handle and turns back to look at me.

"What were you doing when I walked in here?" he asks, catching me off guard.

I force a heavy swallow, not sure what he saw when he walked in, hoping he didn't see me taking pictures.

"I'm not sure that it's any of your business," I snap, "I was changing my clothes."

My voice cracks. I roll my shoulders back, tilting my head to the side, challenging him to push me on it.

If it were anyone else and I didn't have my scholarship on the line, I'd own my sexuality. I've never cared about what people thought of me, and I most definitely don't give a fuck what Ryder thinks either.

Still, I don't want Ryder to suspect I was taking pictures of myself or for word to get out about them being shared with the internet.

"I didn't have anyone here to help me lug my shit from the bus station or up the two flights of stairs. I was freshening up and changing my shirt when you took it upon yourself to bust in here like you own the damn place."

He grits his teeth, clenching his jaw. His face is hard as stone, but his eyes waver, glancing down at my body. He pauses where my crop-top ends, showing off my stomach. My abs tighten from the heat of his stare.

He may be cold as ice toward me and everyone else who tries to get close to him, but those eyes. They tell a different story.

Sooner or later, the cold exterior he carries with him will melt away too.

"You know, this means we're going to be seeing a lot more of each other again."

He shakes his head. His expression unreadable.

"If you're going to convince me you hate me, you'll have to do a better job."

I reach my hand out toward him, dragging my nail across his chest like Aimee had a moment ago. The difference between when she did it to now is we both heard him suck in a deep breath when I did.

His nostrils flare, and I grin at the sight of the subtle tick in his jaw, giving himself away.

It won't be long before Ryder goes back to playing his games, and when he does, I'll be ready.

I'll never let him see me fall.

# Chapter Two

## RYDER

"Son of a motherfucker."

Those are the words I hear as I round the corner of The Grind Café as my cup slams against my chest, splashing all over me.

My lip curls in a snarl, staring down at the large wet spot before my eyes fall on Austen. Her hands are up, her eyes wide, panic shrouding her features.

She's lucky I ditched my coffee for water after my second cup this morning.

"Fuck," she mutters under her breath. "I swear I didn't mean to run into you."

I've seen her twice in a matter of two days since she arrived on campus, and I'm beginning to fear these little run-ins will be a reoccurring thing.

"You always seem to show up wherever I am. Old habits die hard."

Her eyes narrow and her back goes ramrod straight. It's the truth, and she knows it. Back when we were at Haven Brook, Austen always had a way of showing up wherever I was.

"Does your neck ever hurt from carrying around your giant ego?" She tilts her head to the side, full of sass. "Trust me when I say, the last thing I want is to be stuck in your miserable presence."

"Take this as my one and only warning. Stay away from me." I move to pass by her and head back toward my table.

It isn't worth entertaining her or this conversation for a second longer. I have more important things to focus my attention on. I don't have the time, nor the patience, to spend talking to Austen.

She extends her hand out toward me, gripping my arm, stopping me in my tracks. I stare down at where her small fingers hold on to my forearm, noticing the black nail polish on her fingertips.

"Excuse me?" she retorts. "Warning me about what?"

I clench my jaw, my gaze burning into her and her hand.

"Get your hand off me," I say, each word spoken sternly, gritting my teeth.

"What's your problem, Ryder? I haven't done shit to you."

I shrug my arm, yanking it from her hand before gesturing at the front of my shirt.

"Does this look like nothing to you?

"Oh, excuse me, *precious*. I didn't realize a little water would cause you to melt."

I chuckle, looking around the small coffee shop, rubbing my hand over my jaw. The Grind had become my sanctuary of sorts when I needed to get out of my apartment. The walls are empty, the silence is deafening, and I hate being alone with my thoughts.

She might be new on campus, but she needs to be reminded she isn't going to get away with talking to me like this.

"My problem, *princess*, is I don't like when people touch me. You'd do well to remember that too. Next time, why don't you worry about paying attention to where you're going?"

She scoffs and rolls her eyes, crossing her arms over her chest. The move forces her breasts up, accentuating her cleavage. She's dressed in a black shirt with large slits cut into the neckline, a pair of dark denim jeans, and black Vans. I'm trying my hardest not to look, but damn it, I'm a man after all.

"Whatever," she murmurs, rolling her eyes. She moves to adjust the strap of her bag hanging from her shoulder.

She's gotta be fuckin' kidding me. Did she seriously have the nerve to roll her eyes at me?

"In case you forgot who you were talking to, let me remind you, the next time you see me, it would be in your best interest to steer clear of me."

"Got it," she nods, a fake smile flashing on her face. She sucks her lip ring into her mouth, seemingly unfazed by my warning.

She hasn't changed from the first time we met. Even as I stand here and stare at her now, I could rattle off a list of things that remind me of her. All those same reasons are exactly why I made it my mission to steer clear of her. Austen has a way of cutting through all the bullshit and seeing through to the real me. As someone who's worked hard to build a shell around myself, I hate her more because of it.

"Run along now." I wave my hand at her, shooing her away.

"Yeah, yeah. Fuck off." She rolls her eyes again and smirks, strolling past me toward the front of the coffee shop.

My eyes trail behind her as she goes, stirring up the air around us, giving me a whiff of her floral perfume.

If she were any other person, the scent alone would make my dick hard.

I know I have no honest reason for treating her the way I am, but something about her knowing who I was before I moved to Philly makes me want to drive her away. Moving here was supposed to be a fresh start for me. Yet, her showing up and seeing her around is like a flashback to the life we lived when we were younger hitting me square in the jaw.

The only way I could dodge another punch was to do the only thing I could, hit her with a low blow until I knew she'd stay away for good.

Just like the Austen I knew four years ago, she doesn't give a crap what people think of her, much less some piece of shit like me.

I stalk over toward my corner and shove my stuff into my bag, tossing my now empty cup into the garbage behind me. I flash one last look toward Austen as she reaches into her pocket and pulls out her air pods, shoving them into her ears. She evidently lands on a song she likes, her foot and head bobbing in time to the music. Her hair is pulled into one of those messy buns on top of her head with a red bandana, bouncing along with it.

She doesn't give a shit about the hordes of people filing in and out of here, likely coming to and from class. Something about seeing her so carefree captures the attention of people around the room.

I exhale a heavy breath and toss the rest of my stuff in my bag before I slip out the door.

A wall of humidity hits me, the sunshine beaming overhead. I pull out my sunglasses, shielding my eyes from the piercing rays. I reach for my pack of cigarettes and grip the end of my smoke between my lips, flipping the lighter and sucking in a deep inhale.

The sidewalk outside of The Grind is bustling with people coming and going. The small coffee shop is located on campus, making it one of the hot spots for students in between classes.

Despite trying to push it out of my thoughts, my mind keeps drifting back to Austen. Philly isn't far from where we grew up in Cleveland. What are the chances we both ended up here after all this time?

I tilt my head back against the brick wall, holding the cigarette to my mouth, and take another drag. The awning overhead gives a small reprieve from the bright rays before I make the jaunt across campus to my place.

A few minutes later, I watch as Austen rushes out the door, this time with a cup of coffee of her own in her hand. She sidesteps, moving to stand next to me, narrowly missing a group of people walking past the coffee shop.

She doesn't see me right away, but when she turns to look over, her eyes falling on mine, she laughs under her breath and shakes her head.

"Gee precious, you're not gonna help me out at all, are ya?"

"Why the hell would I do you any favors?"

"Oh, I wasn't expecting you to. I was simply saying if you want me to stay away from you, the least you could do is not hang out right outside the door waiting for me."

She holds her phone up, appearing to check the time as she takes a sip of her drink before shoving it back into her pocket.

If she is trying to get under my skin, it is working, when she mimics my stance and leans against the wall next to me.

I release a heavy sigh, which earns me a chuckle.

"You really are too easy to tick off, ya know that?"

I don't even bother responding at this point.

"You do realize now that I'm rooming with your best friend's girlfriend, it's going to make it pretty difficult to avoid me, at least for this year. Next year, you can badger her into working out a transfer or maybe she'll move in with Darren herself. Until then, you might as well suck it up and accept you are once again stuck with me."

"Just because you are roommates doesn't mean I have to be around you. Aimee is stuck on Darren like a leech anyway. She won't have the time for you or whatever friendship you seem to think the two of you have."

"If you say so." She shrugs, taking another drink of her coffee.

She cuts across the busy sidewalk toward the corner, hitting the button for the crosswalk. She stands there, crossing her arms in front of herself before turning her head back toward me, throwing me a wave.

I pretend not to pay her a lick of attention, watching her out of the corner of my eye cross the street and jog toward the radio station.

She double-checks the time on her phone again, shaking her arms and legs out as if releasing pent-up nervous energy. She takes her earbuds out and shoves them into her pocket.

I'm lost in thought watching her, wondering what reason she has for visiting the station, when my phone vibrates in my pocket, pulling me from the questions swirling through my mind.

"Yeah," I answer in greeting.

"Irish," Darren replies gruffly. "The fuck you doin'?"

I take a deep inhale from my cigarette before flicking the end. "Nothin', chillin' outside The Grind."

"Meet me at my place at ten. I'm picking up Aim, and we're heading over to Kappa."

Kappa Sig isn't really my scene, but there are a lot of hot chicks who hang around there. Those rich pricks draw in all sorts of attention with their parents' money and fast cars. I am only lookin' to get my dick wet and drink a little, nothing serious.

It isn't like I have any other plans, and I don't want to spend another night alone at my place, so I take him up on it.

"All right." I reach down to pick up my bag. "I'm gonna head back to my place to get cleaned up. I'll see ya in a bit."

I disconnect the call, neither of us bothering with goodbyes.

I met Darren when I moved to Philly last year. He had connections all over and was friends with a few of the guys in the frat. Although he didn't live with them, his dad was alumni, which meant they considered him one of their own.

I didn't want to ask for the details as to how and why, but I had a feeling he was doing favors for a few of them on the down-low.

You know what they say, "More money, more problems." Those words rang true when it came to Darren. We both grew up running with the wrong crowd. He watched his dad pay off people to do his dirty work, including raising his kid. Ironically enough, now he's the mastermind behind the dirty work. Unlike him, I didn't have the privilege of growing up with money or people looking out for me. Hell, I didn't have a cent to my name when I arrived on campus.

Not until Darren entered the picture anyway. He was there the night I got into it with some prick at one of the frat's bonfires. As soon as he saw me lay the dude out with one punch, he was all too eager to introduce himself and, as the saying goes, the rest is history.

I bet when he got one good look at me, all he saw were dollar signs. I was nothing but a kid with an axe to grind, a fist ready for blows, and a temper looking to release all its aggression.

We were a match made in fucked-up heaven.

My hand is still jacked-up from the last favor I did for Darren. A guy named Rusty owed him some money. I didn't ask questions; I didn't care, to be honest. I was only in it for the payout. The money would be enough to cover me for a while.

He asked me to convince him to cough up the money he owed, and he'd throw a brick my way. All I was going to do was rough him up a bit in hopes it would light a fire under his ass.

Darren knew someone who told him where Rusty had been hanging out. I staked him out for a bit. He must've got wind I was onto him because when I finally went in for it, he was ready for me. He had two of his buddies with him who didn't hesitate to introduce me to their crowbars. My knuckles got crushed in the process, messing up my hand.

Ever since then, I told Darren not to come at me with any of his bullshit.

Don't bring up any fights. Don't ask me to help with a job.

When I left Cleveland, it was with the plan of leaving that life behind.

I adjust the baseball cap on my head to shield my eyes from the sunlight and make a beeline across the street, deciding to take a different route today. I stop outside the radio station, attempting to see through the dark tinted windows along the front. I secretly hope I'll catch another glimpse of Austen, but she's nowhere in sight.

*What the hell are you doing?* I mentally chastise myself.

What did it matter why she was here or what she was up to?

I didn't deserve her or her kindness back then, and I still don't. I was leaving all the bullshit from my past in the rearview mirror the moment I hauled ass out of Cleveland.

Austen included.

# Chapter Three

## AUSTEN

I swipe my palms over the front of my jeans before shaking my hands out, attempting to release the pent-up nervous energy zipping through me.

I've dreamed for years of an opportunity like this to get me out of Cleveland. Everything is finally falling into place better than I could've ever expected.

Well, minus the fact I'm once again forced to deal with Ryder, but I'm not going to let his constant state of doom and gloom ruin my day.

I was on the lengthy list of interested candidates vying over the internship at Rebel radio. It was a long shot, but it's been a dream of mine to work in radio. I'm not going to hold back now.

I could hardly believe it when I heard the news that I got the spot. It was only an internship, for now, which meant I was going to continue posting to my OnlyFun site. I need the money to get me through school, and I don't have the time to add another job into the mix.

Today is my first day at Rebel, and although it didn't start off on the best foot, I refuse to focus on anything else but living in the moment.

I shove my phone and earbuds into my pocket and pull the door open, stepping into the lobby. It's decorated in all black and gray, giving it a modern feel. The radio plays in the seating area, thumping through the speakers.

A desk spans the back wall facing the doors with a Rebel 98.1 logo as the backdrop. A petite redhead peeks her head over the computer screen, greeting me with her warm smile.

"Hi, I'm Austen Fox. I'm the new intern. Can you point me toward Mr. Zeed?"

"Sure thing. It'll be one moment."

When she tilts her head down to pick up the phone, I spot a small dermal piercing near her eye. The diamond glistens beneath the pendant lighting hanging above our heads. She mumbles a few things into the phone before slamming it back down.

"He'll be right out."

A moment later, a man dressed in a pair of black slacks and a green button-up shirt races down the hallway. His energy and megawatt smile only fuels the adrenaline pumping through me.

"Austen." He smiles, extending his hand out to shake mine.

I wince internally, imagining how clammy my hands felt but did my best to cover it up by returning his grin.

"I'm Paul."

He motions for me to follow along, power walking down the hall. I mentally ask him to slow down and take a fuckin' chill pill, nearly jogging to keep up with his pace.

"You couldn't have started at a more perfect time," he says, leading me into a large conference room with boxes covering a long table, stacked one on top of the other.

"We will be kicking off Eastwood's football season at a tailgate event, and we are in desperate need of your help."

He turns to face me, taking a few steps back. I try not to let it show as all my excitement starts to deflate, knowing the first few days aren't going to start quite like I hoped.

*Don't let it get you down.* I mentally tell myself.

We all start somewhere, and if it means doing the bitch work in the beginning, I'll pull up my non-existent sleeves and get to work.

"We'll start by having you unpack these boxes. They are full of bags we'll be loading up with goodies from our sponsors to be handed out to other students at the event."

He continues to give me a rundown of everything I need to do. Just as quickly as he appeared, he's gone, leaving me alone with a list of things to do.

I sigh. "Ahh, well, at least I brought my headphones with me," I mutter, this time out loud.

I manage to get a lot done during my three-hour shift. By the time I leave for the day, I'm beat. The sun is starting to set when I step outside. I make a quick stop for a sandwich and a bag of chips on my hike back to my dorm room.

One of the downsides to being the new kid on campus is not knowing anyone except Aimee.

Well, except for Ryder. Not that it matters anyway. I am nothing more than a stranger to him.

By the time I make the trek up the two flights of stairs to my dorm, I'm ready to crawl into bed and call it a night. I figured Aimee had plans with Darren since she had spent every night with him this week already.

I don't mind, though. I enjoy being alone, and it gives me space to check in with my OnlyFun subscribers without the risk of her getting in my business, which she has a tendency of doing.

The door is unlocked, and I find Aimee sitting on her bed with a mirror leaning against her desk chair and makeup scattered around her. Judging by the large messy bun stacked on top of her head and her half done-up face, she was getting ready to go out somewhere.

"How did your first day go?" she asks, snapping the lid to her compact shut, tossing it onto the pile of stuff next to her.

"Not bad," I sigh, setting my food down on the nightstand. I drop my backpack on the floor and collapse onto my mattress.

"That good, huh?"

"I'm ready to stuff my face then dive right into this pillow." I fling my arm over my eyes, shielding them from the light.

Our dorm is small and noisy, but I can't complain, I've slept in worse places.

If it hadn't been for my journalism teacher, who guided me in the right direction, I wouldn't even be here now.

She was more than my teacher, though, and I'll never be able to repay her for the guidance she gave me growing up.

"Really? On a Friday night? Isn't that a little, I don't know, boring?"

"Ya know, I may decide to go wild and live it up with some *Dateline.*"

She smirks. I sit up and eye her as she dips her finger into her eyeshadow palette and brushes it along her lid.

"You could come out with us, if you want."

"Who is 'us' exactly?"

She pauses, concentrating on her eyeliner. Her mouth open and her tongue out, as if it's going to help her attain expert precision.

"Umm ...I don't know exactly. Me, Darren, and some of his friends. I'm sure Ryder will be there. You know him, right?"

I pull my sandwich out of the bag, unwrapping the paper, and take a heaping bite to avoid making too much out of this conversation. I resort to a nod giving her the information she needs.

She screws the lid on her eyeliner again before her eyes fall on mine.

"I thought you said you were from Cleveland?"

"Yep," I say, in between bites. I'm surprised she doesn't know that about Ryder too.

Well, I wouldn't say surprised is the right word. He isn't exactly the type to be forthcoming about information, especially about his past.

"How do you know Ryder then?" she questions, her face bunching in confusion.

"Long story for another day," I mutter, quickly taking another bite.

She blinks at me, waiting for me to elaborate, but I don't. He's already made it clear he wants nothing to do with me. Lord knows how he'd handle it if he found out I so much as breathed his name or mentioned our upbringing, no matter how brief it may have been.

She reaches for her mascara in the pile and changes the subject.

"There will be quite a few people though. We're hitting up a party over at Kappa Sig. As wild as your night sounds, you should come with us. It'll be a good time. I promise you'll have fun."

I open the bag of chips and toss one into my mouth. I'm not the least bit interested in getting drunk. I don't mind having a few drinks but being under the influence has never been my thing.

The ties that bind me to my past run deep.

"Sure, count me in." I shrug, tossing another chip into my mouth.

I climb up onto my bed, reclining against the wall facing her, watching as she puts the finishing touches on her makeup.

"What are you going to wear?" she asks, as she begins to shove all her stuff back into a makeup bag sitting next to her.

I stare down at my black shirt and denim jeans, peering back up at her.

"What's wrong with what I'm wearing?" I question, tapping the toes of my Vans together.

She takes her hair down, shaking out her long wavy locks. Without warning, she pulls her shirt over her head, tossing it aimlessly toward the laundry basket at the end of her bed before slipping on a little black dress.

It all starts to make sense now.

"Nothing," she sighs. "I guess I just didn't know if you'd want to change is all."

"Nah. The thought of getting all dressed up to hang out with people who have no idea who I am makes me want to stay here with the murderers instead."

"We really are two different people." She laughs.

Isn't that the truth.

I continue to watch her flit around the room getting ready. When she pulls out a pair of four-inch stilettos, it's safe to say her comment was spot on.

You'd never catch me in anything more than a sneaker. I'd end up breaking an ankle.

Two knocks hit our door and, without waiting, Darren barges in. I grit my teeth, already not liking how he seemingly gives no fucks about the fact this is my place too.

"Yes, why don't you come right in and make yourself at home," I blurt out.

Aimee must pick up on the change in my tone, glancing over at me, mouthing "sorry" before turning back to Darren.

He has a beanie pulled low on his head with a black moto jacket on. He shrugs, his eyes gliding over Aimee's body.

I give her a chance to call him out for it, but when she doesn't, I continue.

"There are two people who live here. Next time, don't come walking in here like you own the place."

He chuckles. "Noted."

I have to admit, I do wonder what the heck Aimee sees in him.

He leans his shoulder against the wall, one foot crossed over the other, fingers rapidly tapping on the screen of his phone. Immediately my thoughts drift to Ryder, wondering if it's him he's talking to.

I wouldn't say the way he reacted to running into me at The Grind was at all surprising. In fact, it fit right in with the Ryder I knew from years ago.

I guess I just expected, or maybe hoped is the right word, he had grown up by now and let go of whatever grudge he had with me. I couldn't think of any reason he should have one, though.

Aimee bends down to grab her purse, draping the strap across her body.

"Who are you talking to?" She playfully smacks his arm, a hint of jealousy laced in her words.

"Don't worry about it," he snaps, not bothering to look up or acknowledge the hurt behind her question.

I curl my lip before shoving the last chip in my mouth and climb off my bed.

This guy has a lot of nerve.

"Darren," she quips. "Seriously?"

"Chill. It's just Ryder."

He smirks, returning to his text. This guy is a jackass. At no time, in the history of ever, has telling a woman to "chill" worked.

"You ready? I want to go." He shoves his phone back in his pocket, seeming disinterested when his eyes fall on her.

She nods, following behind him.

I'm beginning to wish I declined the offer after all.

Something about the tension and bickering between the two of them feels like a preview of what's to expect the next time I run into Ryder.

*Great.*

# Chapter Four

## RYDER

The music at Kappa is blaring. The level of bass thumping through the speakers sends my adrenaline racing. I'm ready for a beer to loosen me up.

I duck my head and weave through the crowd. It's packed tonight. I almost regretted coming when I saw the number of people here. Any lingering doubt confirms it when my eyes fall on Austen. She's standing near the corner of the living area, clutching a red solo cup in her hand. Her eyes scan the room of people, shock and annoyance evident on her face.

I can't contain the urge to laugh. She's always been one to wear what she was thinking. You could sort through her every thought and feeling simply by studying her expression.

Her eyes drop over to the two girls standing in front of her, both with drinks in their hands. Her brows shoot up when one bends over, grinding against the other. They're both clearly not paying attention when beer sloshes over the side of their cups, spilling all over themselves and the floor.

Austen shakes her head and laughs, taking a long pull from her drink. Her eyes catch mine through the hordes of people.

I should be annoyed she once again was showing up where she didn't belong or for encroaching on my territory. Although something about seeing her less than impressed reaction, knowing she feels the same way I do about being crammed in a tight space with all these uppity assholes, makes me smile.

"What up, bro?" Darren asks, cutting through the crowd, pulling my attention away from Austen.

"Nothin'." I shoulder past him to the keg of beer. I reach for one of the cups near the cooler, adjusting my grip and fill it up.

"How's your hand?" He gestures toward my banged-up knuckles before lifting his beer to his mouth. He's asked me the same question for months and he's heard the same answer every time.

I roll my eyes and shake my head. "Whatever you're thinking, you can forget it."

"Listen, Irish, do you realize what you're doing? You are missing out on rollin' in some serious change right now."

"Dude, I don't give a shit. All right? I told you I was done, so quit bringing it up."

He chuckles and shakes his head.

It's no secret I grew up poor. He thinks he can convince me to do his dirty work by throwing out talk of money. He gets a cut of each of my fights in the ring. As for setting me up with whatever associates he has, I have no idea, but I know he likely sees a cut there too.

Either way, there is always something in it for him, and I want nothing to do with the bullshit anymore.

"Whatever. Whenever you decide to quit milkin' that pussy, you let me know."

"Excuse me?" I turn toward him, pressing my hand against his chest, and shove him into the crowd.

He eats it up, a sinister grin stretching wide across his face, unfazed. He wouldn't be smiling if he was the target for my fists, but he knows I'd never stoop to his level.

I smirk and shake my head.

He turns and pulls Aimee into his arms before they're swallowed up by the crowd.

When I toss a glance in Austen's direction, I'm surprised when I find her near the corner, only this time, she has company.

I knew who it was the moment my eyes caught his shaggy blond hair. He was a member of the frat and one of the cockiest motherfuckers I'd ever met. His dad was made of money and they had a tendency of using it to throw their weight around. He was no stranger to The Ring. At one point, I was itching to meet him there, just to get my hands on him.

Out of all the guys on campus, I wouldn't have expected Austen to be so dumb to even entertain a conversation with him.

I move back toward the outside of the room, already sick of the number of people here and the strong smell of alcohol mixed with sweat. It's another reminder of why I hate these parties.

Although they always seem to bring in some of the hottest chicks, they bring in a lot of trash too. I don't even think most of these people are students here; most are looking for a party and a place to crash at the end of the night.

I lean against the wall, bending my leg beneath me. I take a heavy gulp of beer and push the thought of Austen and Justin out of my mind.

I stare off into the swarm of people thrusting and grinding against one another. The lights are dim above, but through the sea of bodies, I spot a girl moving through the crowd toward me. Her name is Jenna. I grin, recalling the last time I saw her. She is a sweet girl, but when the door shut and the lights went out, it brought out another side of her entirely.

Her eyes light up when she sees me, and I take another drink of my beer to hide my grin.

Something about the move has my eyes darting over to Austen. In the same moment, her eyes peer over Justin's shoulder and meet mine before snapping away.

I don't care. If she's into watching, I'll let her.

When my eyes meet Jenna's once again and those hot ass lips walk toward me, I push all thoughts of Austen out of my mind, recalling the way Jenna's mouth felt wrapped around me.

"Ryder." She smirks as if reading my thoughts.

When she finally reaches me, I get a good look at her. She is dressed in a pair of denim shorts, showing off her sculpted legs, with a red corset top. The material cinches tight, lifting her breasts to the point they nearly spill over.

"Jenna." I tilt my head toward her.

She takes a step toward me, our chests brushing against one another, and traces her long fingernail over the ridges of my stomach. She continues her path south, pausing for a moment before she drags her nail over the outline of my dick pressed against the front of my pants.

She quirks her brow, challenging me. I know she is waiting for me to take control while relishing in her chance to tease me.

"It's been a while since we …" she trails off, smiling.

I reach for her ponytail, twisting the long locks in my hand, tilting her head back. Her eyelids fall, her teeth raking over her bottom lip. She loves it, and the small moan she shutters against my ear confirms it.

A tingle races through my body, urging me to look over at Austen. I know without checking, her eyes are on me, watching me with Jenna.

Jenna's hand cups my dick, growing hard in my pants. I adjust my grip on her hair when she turns, pressing her tight ass against me. I stare down between us as she rocks against me.

This time I'm unable to avoid the temptation, and I peer over at Austen. Her eyes are burning into my front where Jenna is grinding against me. My breath is nearly caught in my throat.

When she notices me looking at her, she flashes me a wink and lifts her cup in the air before taking a drink.

Justin moves to stand next to her, noticing something has caught her attention. He stops talking and follows her line of sight.

His lips curl in a sneer when he sees me, tilting his head from side to side as if he were challenging me from across the room.

As much as I'd love to lay his ass out, he isn't worth a second of my time.

My hatred for Justin runs deeper than my dislike for Austen. She's new here, so she likely hasn't heard the talk about him. I'd like to think if she had, she wouldn't be entertaining a conversation with him.

Rumors have been swirling around about him getting a little too handsy with women, and his ego doesn't know how to take being rejected.

I shake my head, not giving him a second more of my time.

Jenna must notice my attention is no longer on her; she turns to face me, pushing against my chest.

I peer down at her, reaching my arm out to pull her back when she smacks mine away.

I don't have time for the games. If she wants to be that way, she can bounce herself and those fake tits out of here.

"You can be such an asshole," she shouts over the music, stepping between my legs once more.

"I may have been told that a time or two," I grunt. "I'm not going to chase after you. If you want to be in my bed, I'll take you back to my place and fuck you until you scream. That's all it will ever be, though."

The mention of fucking her again has a darkness falling over her eyes, her lids lowering with desire.

I have her right where I want her, that's if I still want her.

Yet, I can't deny the urge to look in Austen's direction again. The lights grow dimmer, making it hard to see her. Aimee's still nowhere to be found.

It ticks me off that she brought Austen here and then dipped out, leaving her alone with a room of strangers.

Justin slips into the crowd. When Austen notices him gone, she makes a beeline in the opposite direction, weaving through the crowd of people right toward me.

"I'll need a rain check," I shout over the music to Jenna.

"Are you fuckin' kiddin' me?" She scoffs.

"Go," I spit out.

"Fuck off." She raises her finger behind her.

I was standing near the doorway, so if Austen were looking to cut out of here, she'd have to walk by me first. I lean against the wall and wait for her to approach me.

She keeps her eyes forward, pretending as though I'm not here.

"Where you off to, princess?" I holler.

She grits her teeth, coming to a stop in front of me.

"Don't worry about it," she throws back without hesitation.

I narrow my eyes at her. Her gaze takes in my face, pausing on my mouth where my jaw clenches.

What is it about her that gets under my skin like no one else?

"Did Big Boobs McGee bail when she found out you weren't packin' like she thought?"

My nostrils flare. She loves pushing my buttons. Judging by the way her grin stretches across her face, she thought she was fuckin' clever with that joke.

I take a step toward her, eliminating the distance separating us, and bend down so I am close enough for her to hear.

"Are you jealous?"

She rears back and smacks her hand over her mouth to cover her laugh.

I knew she was watching when I wrapped my hand in Jenna's hair. I reach my hand out and grip the back of her neck, pulling her close to me.

"Don't fuck with me, Austen," I grunt.

Any laughter coming from her is silenced in that moment. Her hand falls to her side.

When she tilts her head back enough to look me in the eye, something shifts in her gaze. It reminds me of the girl I met years ago when she showed up in the middle of the night at Haven Brook.

"I warned you to stay away from me."

"You should know your taunts and empty threats don't mean shit to me."

"I'm not the same kid you knew back then."

Her eyes shift, burning into the scar over my brow bone. I can practically see the questions swirling around in her mind.

"Neither am I."

I smirk, releasing my grip.

"The difference between you and me is I don't try to hide who I am. I don't chase away my demons anymore. I run with them."

"Oh, so really you're just trying to prove how big of an asshole you are? Got it." She waves her hand at me. "Good luck with that."

She makes it two steps past me before I grab her forearm and pull her with me into a small alcove. It's meant to be a coat closet but it's more the size of a small bedroom.

"What are you doing?" She huffs, her eyes darting around the dark room.

She takes a step away, pressing her back against the wall. Her chest heaves, releasing a heavy exhale.

"Ryder," she moans out my name.

I don't know what I'm thinking or what has come over me. I can't blame it on alcohol, but something about being near her is intoxicating all on its own.

I tilt my head down into the crux of her neck, inhaling the scent of her perfume mixed with sweat.

Neither of us cross the line into touching again.

"Admit you were jealous."

"No."

I chuckle. It is low and throaty, causing her to shift her legs from side to side.

"Did you wish it was me touching you?"

"No."

"Were you jealous watching her stroke my dick through my jeans?"

Her lip curls and she exhales slowly. "No."

"Did you think about what it would be like if I were gripping your hair from behind while I fucked you?"

"Ryder." She sighs as she says my name.

"Say it."

"Maybe ..." Her words trail off.

I step back and reach into my pocket to pull out my pack of cigarettes. I lift one to my mouth, flicking my lighter open to ignite the end.

I keep the flame lit between us, enough for her to get a better look at my face.

"You can get the thought out of your mind, princess. I wouldn't touch you if you were the last pussy left on this campus."

Without another word, I stride past her and out of the closet, hoping this time she'll heed my warning and stay the hell away from me.

# Chapter Five

## AUSTEN

The days that followed the party at Kappa Sig were spent chipping away at the mountain of homework and studying I had to do while trying to keep my mind off Ryder.

It seems like everywhere I go since arriving on campus has been tied to him in some way or another.

The shrill sound of my alarm clock ringing from my nightstand causes me to groan, blindly reaching out to grab my phone to shut it up.

"Make it stop," Aimee grumbles from her side of the room.

I peek my head out from under my covers and quickly fumble with my phone before hitting the button to stop the alarm.

I heard Aimee amble through the door early this morning. I was up until after midnight when I fell asleep watching Netflix.

I push myself up and rake my fingers through my hair, massaging my scalp. Aimee is still dressed in her outfit from the night before, one leg hanging off the side of her bed.

*At least she took off her shoes.*

I still have a crap ton of homework left and need to find time to record content for my OnlyFun website. I work today at the station, but after that, I have the next three days off, giving me time to try and get caught up.

I decide to quickly shower and get ready before mustering up the energy to head to The Grind for coffee. I desperately need a shock to my system only coffee can provide if I have any hope of getting anything done today. I shove all my books into my bag and make the quiet walk across campus. I was expecting it to be more alive this morning, but I guess most of the students aren't anxious to crawl out of bed.

The bell chimes when I pull the door open, joining the long line of students waiting for their fix.

My mind drifts back to the last time I was here when I ran into Ryder, then to the night at the Kappa Sig party. I'm replaying my conversation with Ryder when behind me, the sound of a throat clearing breaks through my thoughts. I turn and find Justin standing there with his hands in his pockets, flashing me a warm smile.

He's an attractive guy but the opposite of Ryder in so many ways. Where Ryder's hair is shaved, Justin's is longer on the top. It has a ruffled look to it, almost as if he had woken up like this. Ryder is always dressed in dark colors, which is something we have in common. Justin is clean-cut.

I can't help but wonder what it is he sees in me.

It isn't like I know many people around here, and he's always going out of his way to show he cares. Although I'm not sure where he sees this going or what he wants exactly, I'm not going to push him away either.

He also hasn't warned me to stay away, like the resident asshole on campus.

"Why'd you take off the other night? When I came back, you had disappeared. Aimee said you went back to your dorm."

"Yeah." I sigh. "Sorry about that. It was a long day, and I was ready to get home and crash."

He stares at me for a long second, almost as if reading into my response to gauge whether he believes me.

"I should've said goodbye first," I follow up, attempting to reassure him it wasn't personal.

"S'all good." He smiles. "Listen, we're having a bonfire tomorrow night out at Greencastle. It's basically a field outside of town where a bunch of us go to drink and have a good time. You should come."

"Go to some random field out in the middle of nowhere?" I question.

He must sense my suspicion, but I don't care. I've seen enough crime documentaries to know how this story ends.

"I know how it sounds, but I swear, it's legit. Ask Aimee. She's probably going anyway. I've seen her there with Darren and Ryder many times."

The mention of Ryder going has me wanting to back out before I push the thought from my mind.

I'm not going to avoid going out with friends simply for the sake of avoiding him. He can't run me away with his bullshit taunts and warnings.

"Yeah, it sounds like a good time."

He pulls out his phone, his fingers moving quickly over the screen.

"Go ahead and save your number and I'll message you tomorrow night."

He hands his phone over and I type my number into his contacts. When I move to pass the phone back to him, his hand brushes mine, caressing the skin along the back. He stares down at my outstretched arm. I expect him to make a comment on the wildflowers tattoo covering my forearm, like I often hear, but he doesn't.

I pull my arm back, feeling self-conscious under his scrutinizing stare. The tattoo means a lot to me; it's something I got for my eighteenth birthday.

He waits with me while we both order our drinks and joins me on the walk across the street over to the radio station.

"I should probably head inside." I smile, motioning to the building.

"All right," he says as he glances at the building before his eyes meet mine. "I'll text you later. You can chat with Aimee and let me know if you want to hit up the bonfire. We can always find something else to do instead if you want."

"Sounds good." I turn and reach for the handle. I flash him a smile and a wave before ducking inside.

It's only my second day, and I don't want to be late already.

They still have me helping with the upcoming event, which is fun because it passes the time, even though I am dying to get in and learn about the production process.

"Good work today," Paul says, just as I am picking up before I leave. "We'll have you start to learn more of the ropes next week. I know you're eager to get in the studio, and don't worry, you will soon."

I'm riding a high as I leave and make the walk back to my dorm. It's still early, just after four o'clock, so I'm happy to have the night free.

Aimee is sitting at her desk when I walk in, shocking the hell out of me. It's the first time I've seen her do anything since we started rooming together that remotely resembles focusing on school. You would've thought her sole purpose for being here was to hang out with Darren and hit up all the best parties.

"Oh, hey." She turns in her seat, resting her arm along the back of her chair. "There was some man here earlier. He was older, wearing a suit. Looked important. Anyway, he was looking for you and asked me to give you this."

She hands me an envelope with my name printed on the front. I stare at it, brows furrowing. There is no return address, just my name.

"Did he say who he was or why he was looking for me?"

"No. He just said it was urgent and stressed making sure you got this." She shrugs.

I drop my bag at the end of my bed and kick off my shoes, taking a seat on the edge of the mattress. I hesitate for a second, running my finger under the lip of the envelope and pull out the paper inside.

The letter is addressed from a lawyer out of Cleveland, sending the hairs on my neck standing in attention. Only a handful of people know where I am, although it isn't like I was trying to hide either.

I guess there aren't many people who I thought would go looking for me anyway.

My eyes scan over the letter. The further I read, the more the unease twists in my stomach like a knot.

"Are you okay?" Aimee asks. "What's it say?"

I don't respond, reaching into my back pocket for my phone. I quickly type in the number listed along the bottom of the paper.

The phone rings twice before a woman answers. "Hello, thank you for calling Morio Law Offices. How can I help you?"

Her voice was sweet.

"I'm sorry, umm …" My mind goes blank, still trying to digest what I just read. "Can I speak to Mr. Morio, please?"

"May I ask who's calling?"

"Austen," my voice croaks. "Austen Fox."

"One moment." I hear a clicking sound before the line goes silent. I'm thankful they don't keep me on hold with some upbeat jazz music, giving me a second to sort through my thoughts.

Out of the corner of my eye, I notice Aimee move from her desk to sit on her bed across from me. She must sense the change in my mood, or maybe she could hear the conversation on the other line; I can't be sure.

A few seconds later, the line picks back up, and the kind voice is replaced with a gruff, older man.

"This is Clint Morio," he says matter-of-factly.

"Yes, hello. Uh, this is Austen Fox. I received a letter in the ..." I want to say mail but that isn't true. "I received a letter today, and I'm returning your call."

"Austen, yes. I've been trying to reach you for some time now."

My stomach rolls, wondering where this conversation is going.

"I'm sure you've read over the letter and know this is about your father."

The mention of the man, or rather my sperm donor, causes my lip to curl. I wouldn't call him my father by any stretch of the imagination, but if you were to ask my mother, I'm sure she'd say she feels differently.

"Yes. What is this about exactly? I haven't spoken to him in over five years."

If I'm being truthful, I wouldn't mind if I went another five more without hearing from him too.

"I'm sorry to be the one to inform you of this. I understand your mother is, uh, unavailable at this time."

I press my lips together to smother my laugh, not wanting to further delay him from getting to the damn point already. She's unavailable because she's in prison, leaving very few people left to have whatever conversation he is about to have with me.

"Your father has passed away."

If I were to make a list of reasons why he'd be calling me, this wouldn't have made the top five. I'm not sure how I should respond to hearing those words, but surprise is intermixed in there somewhere. He was a powerful man. Many people in his life would be upset hearing the news.

I, on the other hand, can't find it in me to care. Maybe that makes me cruel, but it is the truth. He doesn't deserve an ounce of my sympathy, which is good because I don't have anything in me left to give to him.

"Okay," I said, not sure how to respond. "What does this matter have to do with me exactly?"

"He suspected you'd feel this way."

I bet he did. Which makes the reason why Mr. Morio is calling me now even more confusing.

"I was hoping you could come by my office soon to discuss this matter in person."

"Discuss what exactly?"

"Your father left behind a will, entitling you to a sizable portion of his estate."

"His estate?" I laugh. It is loud, almost maniacal. "What the hell does he think I want with his estate?"

Of course, he would think he could throw money at me after he died, and it would be like all his sins were forgiven. After all, it seemed to work when he did the same to my mother.

"Would you be able to come by my office next week on the sixteenth to discuss this matter in person? We will be settling the estate."

"What if I say no? There's nothing he could've left for me that I would possibly want."

"I think if you were to come and sit down with me, you might feel differently about this matter, Ms. Fox."

I want to roll my eyes. I'm gripping the phone in my hand until my knuckles turn white.

"The money from your inheritance alone is valued at one million dollars."

My eyes nearly bulge out of my eye sockets.

*One million dollars.*

"I'll have to get back to you," I say, not sure what to say next. "Thank you for your time."

Before he has a chance to respond, I disconnect the line and let the phone drop between my legs onto the floor.

I simply have no words for him, or for my father.

# Chapter Six

## AUSTEN

"Ahh, shit."

I don't notice the door open until I hear Ryder mutter the word under his breath. I'm bent forward, lacing up my black combat boots.

I drop my foot to the ground and press my hands to my legs to stand. Ryder's eyes lock on mine as I do, but when they momentarily drop down to take in what I'm wearing, I hear him suck in a quick breath.

My, my, my. How the tables have turned.

His jaw is unhinged, and his gaze burns into me, and I can't help but smirk. This is precisely why I opted to wear this outfit. Well, because I know I look hot as fuck, not because I want a reaction out of him.

I'm dressed in my favorite pair of dark denim jeans with rips along the front of my thigh with a black lace bodysuit underneath. It fits me like a glove, the straps crossing over my chest, making my tits look amazing.

"Can I help you?" I break through the silence.

It seems to shake him from his daze, bringing back the familiar asshole I know and hate.

"Aimee told me to meet her and Darren here."

"I didn't think that meant walking in like you own the place, but welcome." I hold my hand out like I'm Vanna fuckin' White.

I drop my hands to my waist, adjusting my pants. His eyes fall to where my hands are as if he's half expecting me to drop them that very second at the sight of him.

I pull my hair out of my ponytail, shaking out the long brown locks, letting them fall into waves around me.

"You goin' out tonight?" he questions.

I find it interesting he bothers to ask, but if he wants to drop his act, I'll let it go too.

"Yeah."

I reach into Aimee's makeup bag she left sitting by the mirror. She told me I could use any of it whenever I want. I tend to stick to moisturizer and mascara, but I decide to spice it up tonight with some eyeliner.

"I have a date tonight." I peer up beneath my lashes at Ryder. I wouldn't consider it a date, but I'm looking for a reaction from him more than anything.

His brows dart up and he nods, trying and failing to cover up the look of shock and disappointment on his face.

"You and Justin are getting pretty serious then, huh?"

I want to laugh as I unscrew the cap of the eyeliner and turn toward the mirror. His eyes rake over my body as if taking in the view before they meet mine.

"Definitely not serious."

He nods, taking a seat on Aimee's bed.

"Did Aimee say where she was at? She made it seem like she wasn't coming back here before she went to the bonfire."

"She was over at Darren's. They were grabbing a few things from his place but told me to meet them back here."

I know Aimee, and a part of me wonders if she's plotting out an attempt to get the two of us alone. She has brought up my past with Ryder a few times since the night of the Kappa Sig party, mentioning how she could see the two of us together. I didn't waste any time letting her know that would never happen.

I've been practicing doing my eyeliner the past few days after watching Aimee several times. I swipe my finger beneath my eye to wipe away where it smeared before reaching for my mascara.

I can feel Ryder's eyes on me the entire time I do.

"I didn't know you wore makeup."

"I didn't know you cared enough to notice, or hell, even bother to point it out," I say, calling him out.

"Didn't say I cared."

"Didn't say I wanted to hear it either," I retort.

He huffs out a breath. Yeah, you're exhausting me too, idiot.

I finish my mascara, dropping it with the rest of my stuff into the bag before running my hand through my hair. I reach into my pocket for my phone and snap a couple pictures to share with my subscribers tonight.

My eyes fall on Ryder, following him in the mirror as he moves across the room, coming to stand behind me.

"I wasn't trying to be rude." His voice is low, and for a second, I almost wonder if I heard him correctly.

"If that's true, you have an odd way of showing it."

"I'm talking about tonight." He exhales, shaking his head before turning to walk away.

"No, wait." I stop him.

He's trying to be nice and I'm continuing to push his buttons.

"It's just, one second you're hot and then the next you're cold. I can't keep up."

He turns back toward me, moving to take a step closer.

"What I was trying to say was you don't need makeup. You're beautiful without it."

His eyes dip down to the tattoo on my forearm, lifting my arm to study the design.

"Wildflowers?" he asks.

I wonder if he recognizes the design. His thumb brushes over my skin, skating down toward my wrist. I exhale slowly, trying to control my heart rate from his touch alone.

I nod. "They are strong and resilient. It's my reminder you can grow through anything."

We lock eyes in the reflection of the mirror. I press my lips into a thin line, surprised by the change in his demeanor. I'm afraid if I say anything, he'll swing in the other direction, shifting back to being cold and cruel.

He takes me off guard when he moves in closer, sweeping my hair out of my face, leaving my shoulder and neck exposed.

He pauses, waiting for me to stop him. The closer he gets, the harder it is for me to think about anything other than his body pressed against mine.

He takes a deep breath. "Fuck, you smell good."

A grin stretches across my face, and he shakes his head as if trying to push the thought out of his mind.

"He doesn't deserve you," he whispers.

"Is that what this is about? You're only saying this so, what, I won't go out on the date with him?"

He exhales, scrunching his brows together. "Do you truly want to?"

"Ryder …"

He sighs, shaking his head. "Forget it."

He grips my hip and turns me to face him.

"What I'm trying to say is you look beautiful. You always look beautiful," he says.

He reaches his hands out, trailing his fingers over my hips, pushing me until my back is pressed against the closet door. The coolness from the mirror feels good through the sheer material against my warm skin.

My body trembles from his touch, sending goose bumps breaking out over my arms.

He lifts his hand, tracing his thumb along my bottom lip.

I can't remember the last time I kissed a man, much less felt anything compared to what I'm feeling now. He has barely touched me, yet I can't shake the heat spreading through my body and the desire pooling low in my belly.

I knew from seeing him with Big Boobs McGee he was experienced when it came to knowing his way around a woman's body.

I try my best to push all thoughts of them together, or any other girl on campus for that matter, out of my mind. He brushes his finger over my lower lip before he bends down, his mouth only a millimeter away from mine. I suck in a sharp breath, waiting for him to kiss me. I reach my hands out, gripping his forearms, attempting to steady myself while desperately needing to hold on to him before I crumble to the floor.

"Kiss me," I whisper, not wanting him to wait any longer.

It is all the permission he needs before his lips crash down on mine. Everything moves in slow motion from there. A moan escapes my mouth, and the energy from the kiss alone buzzes through me, rocking me to my core.

I can hardly comprehend how this is happening between us.

Ryder fuckin' O'Rourke is kissing me.

If I allow myself to overthink it anymore, I am going to recoil and pull back from him, letting the questions swirling through my head take over and ruin the moment.

Instead, I push it all aside and let myself feel.

His hands trace a path over my hips, his fingers burning into my skin.

Ryder is nearly a foot taller than me, so when I slip my hands around his neck, he grips my thighs in his strong hands, hoisting me up and pinning my back against the wall.

This move is dangerous for both of us.

I trail my tongue over the seam of his lips, scratching my nails over his scalp, earning me a growl.

We break apart, and he presses his forehead to mine, both of us struggling to catch our breath.

When I tilt my head back to look him in the eye, I search his face for any signs he wants to stop, but there are none. A smile lines the corners of my mouth, and I bite down on my lower lip before tipping his chin back up to me.

His grip on my thighs never wanes, rocking his hips to thrust his hard length against me. The move creates a delicious friction over my clit, and I grind against him, giving back to him as much as he's giving me.

"Shit," he mutters when he pulls back from my lips.

A second later, the sound of keys jiggling in the lock interrupts us, and he quickly sets me back on my feet.

My legs are like jelly beneath me, and I hold my hand out to steady myself against my dresser. My gaze darts over to Ryder, and he quickly steps back from me. Aimee pushes the door open, hitting Ryder in the arm in the process.

"Motherfucker," he curses under his breath, catching Aimee off guard.

She and Darren are standing in the doorway, her keys in one hand, purse in the other. Her eyes bounce between Ryder and over to me.

I don't know if my makeup is messed up, but judging by the look on her face, it's safe to say we are busted.

"What's going on? What were you two doing?"

"He was fixing the door to the closet," I lie.

Just as Ryder says, "Nothin'."

Aimee raises her brow, and I know we're caught.

"Which one is it? He was fixing the door, or you were doing nothing?" Aimee smirks, clearly enjoying razzing us.

A text message dings on my phone and I use the distraction to check who it's from.

"I gotta go. My ride is here."

"Justin?" Aimee asks, her tone changing to one of surprise.

I can sense Ryder's gaze burning into me. The urge to look at him is killing me, but I know if I do, I'll be tempted to cancel with Justin entirely.

I don't want to do that, mostly because I'm not convinced this whole thing isn't a dream.

"Yeah. You're still going to Greencastle, right?"

She nods, her eyes peering over to look at Ryder, and I do the same. He's busy typing away on his phone. It's as if everything that happened between us a moment ago never occurred.

"All right, well, I guess we'll see you there."

I reach for my keys and ID, slipping them into my pockets along with my phone. I'm not the type of girl who carries a purse.

I chance one last glance in Ryder's direction, silently wishing he'd look at me, wanting him to know this date with Justin means nothing. Not like the kiss we shared did.

"See you guys there."

Aimee nods as I pass by her and Darren out the door.

It isn't until I step out into the hall, pulling the door shut behind me, when I hear Ryder say, "Fuck, I can't wait to get laid tonight."

It looks like we both made a mistake tonight.

Although I'm not sure ours were the same.

# Chapter Seven

## RYDER

As soon as the door shuts behind Austen, I can practically see the questions swirling through Aimee's mind.

"Want to tell me what we just walked in on?"

"Nothin'."

My response is curt. If she thinks she's going to get anything else from me, she is out of her damn mind. I know Aimee. She likes to open her big mouth. If she found out about our kiss, there's no telling who she'd run and blab her mouth to.

"Did she tell you about her dad?"

The sudden change in our conversation throws me off. "Her dad?"

I didn't know much about him, honestly. Only what the rumor mill circulated back at Haven Brook, which was hardly a reliable source.

"What about him?"

"I guess he took a ride to the other side."

She says it so nonchalantly it sends Darren into a coughing fit, nearly choking on air. She shrugs, clearly not finding anything wrong with her cold way of saying Austen's dad passed away. She shuffles through her bag of tricks Austen was rummaging through before putting that shit on her face she doesn't need.

"She got a letter in the mail the other day. Something about an inheritance. Guess he left her some money she wants nothing to do with."

Why am I not surprised?

One of the rumors that went around about her was how she had come from money. She liked to play it off like she didn't, which made people think it was because she was spoiled. She always talked like she had it rough, but I could see through her bullshit.

When we pull up to Greencastle a short while later, I'm surprised to find more people here than the times before. I chalk it up to word getting out about the bonfires to freshmen who are eager to hit up the best parties.

Darren is rambling off details about an upcoming fight, but I can't find it in me to care enough to focus on the conversation.

He's trying to convince me to get back in the ring. As much as I'd love the chance to take out some pent-up aggression, I have no interest in it anymore.

Darren works on the down-low for some of the richest and most powerful men in Philly. People don't talk about it, mostly out of fear, but I know there's more to why he's kept pressuring me to get back in the ring. How else does he manage to find old, abandoned warehouses spur the moment for last-minute fights?

My fights had been some of the top events, raking in some serious dough. Although he is looking out for me as his friend, I know he's also thinking about the financial gains for himself.

He continues to drone on and on while my gaze focuses on the fire, my attention drifts back to pinning Austen against the wall. The delicious roll of her hips grinding on my dick had me harder than I could ever remember being.

Her subtle moans vibrating against my lips, her fingers digging into my skin as she held on to me.

I wanted so badly to carry her over to her bed and rip her pants off, explore her wet heat. I find myself imagining how tight she'd be when I slid into her for the first time.

I hated Aimee and Darren for choosing that moment to walk through the door and Justin for following behind them, or for even showing up at all. One minute she was here, and another she was gone, walking into the arms of someone else.

Every few minutes, my gaze does a quick sweep over the crowd, although it's hard to see in the darkness. The only light comes from the two bonfires in the field positioned side by side with people gathered around each of them.

"Austen!" Aimee shouts.

I spot the battered old pickup truck pull up a few feet away. When he cuts the engine, the headlights go with it. My gaze locks on Austen, who's staring back at me through the windshield.

It dawns on me how ironic it is for Justin to be showing up here in a truck like this when he works for his dad's dealership, giving him the hookup.

My eyes dart back to Aimee's, where she's sitting on the other side of the bench seat made from a large log facing the fire.

A group of people is huddled near the front of Justin's truck, but they disperse and the crowd parts as they head toward where we're sitting. Justin walks behind Austen, pressing his hand to her lower back, guiding her over to the log facing us.

My eyes trail down her body, taking in every curve beneath her tight outfit. My fingers itch to feel her soft skin against mine.

She's only been here for a couple of weeks, yet I'm already crumbling under the weight of how much I want her.

My gaze lingers where Justin touches her, and I lift my cup of beer to my mouth, needing something to distract me before I say something I'll regret later.

She's always pushing my buttons, and this is yet another way she is dead set on driving me wild.

She takes a seat across from me, Justin following suit, taking the spot next to her. She talks animatedly to Aimee before her eyes flick over to mine.

Darren must sense the change in my mood and drops the conversation about the fight altogether.

Justin eyes me from across the fire, noticing the tension building between the two of us. When's he going to get a clue? I'm two seconds away from laying his ass out, but for what reason?

*She's not worth it. Let it go.*

When he moves his hand around her waist and leans in to whisper in her ear, I could swear her body begins to tremble. After that, all I can see is red.

"Who wants to play a game of Truth or Dare?" Aimee asks.

I glance over at her, and she raises a brow, tempting me.

"How fuckin' old are we?" I mutter, lifting my beer to take another heavy swallow.

If I'm going to deal with childish bullshit all night, I want to be smashed out of my mind.

"Austen, you in?" Aimee presses.

"Yeah …" she trails off, her gaze finding mine. "Sure, why not?"

"You're up first then. Truth or Dare?"

She shrugs. "Truth."

I sneer. Of course, she would.

"Okay then … truth. What's your history with Ryder?"

She is in the middle of taking a drink of her own when her eyes bounce over to mine.

I raise my brow, curious how she's going to answer. It's not like it's a big deal, but we both know people won't understand either.

It is the questions that always seem to follow that I hate answering.

"Never mind. Dare."

Justin's brows furrow and his eyes bounce from her back to me, realizing there is more between us than he knew. I grin, flashing him a wink wanting to get under his skin.

"All right then, dare. I dare you to kiss Ryder again."

"What the hell, Aimee?" Austen scoffs.

"What? It's just a game. Quit gettin' your panties all in a twist. Jesus!" Aimee fires back.

Austen glances over at Justin before her eyes fall to the ground. Her lips are moving, appearing to say something under her breath to him. He nods and she stands, looking back at me, accepting her fate.

I do the same, tracking her as she walks around the fire toward me. Her eyes narrow, clearly pissed. She can be mad all she wants, but she's doing it.

I grip her hips and pull her close to me. I faintly hear Justin mutter, "What the fuck" but it doesn't stop me.

"Try to pretend like you hate me, princess."

"Fuck you," she says, fighting off the grin curving the edge of her mouth.

Her body molds perfectly against mine. I lean forward and tilt her mouth up toward me. I pause just before our lips meet and a small smile peeks through again. A swarm of catcalls and whistles shrill around us, but I tune them out the moment my lips meet hers.

When I open my mouth, my tongue brushes over the seam of her lips, and I swear I feel her body shudder against mine.

She takes a step away, breaking the kiss, and lifts the back of her hand to her mouth, wiping her lips. She can act like she didn't enjoy it, but even I don't miss the desire glazing her eyes.

She rakes her teeth over her lower lips. I swear I can see the hint of blush warming her skin.

She shakes her head and stalks back toward Justin.

I tell myself she was only playing it off like she didn't want it with Aimee and the crowd of people around us. We both know it wasn't even an hour ago she was desperately clawing at me, telling me to kiss her.

"Keep pretending like you didn't like it!" I shout back at her.

Justin's head snaps over to me, shooting daggers my way. I notice the gash on his forehead before he shakes his hair to cover it back up.

"Your turn, Austen."

She focuses her attention back on Aimee. The flare in her eyes warning her she's out for revenge.

"Aimee. Truth or Dare?"

"Truth."

"Other than Darren, have you ever had an inappropriate dream about any of the guys here?"

She shakes her head and rolls her eyes.

"Duh. Sorry, Darren, you know I love you, but there isn't a person here with eyes or a vagina who hasn't thought about fucking Ryder ten different ways."

"I'm down if you're down," I joke, knowing how easy it is to get under Darren's skin.

"I will kill you," he grunts, shoving me.

His response sends both me and Aimee into a fit of laughter, knowing he's right. I don't doubt I could lay Darren out if it were a battle between our fists, but he fights dirty. If he wanted to, he'd take care of the job, and he'd find someone to do it, so he wouldn't have to break a sweat.

"Guess it's my turn again," Aimee grins, holding her hands up, tapping her fingers together as if plotting something devious.

"Ryder."

I know wherever she is going with this will be interesting. She wants me to say dare, which is why I am flipping the script on her.

"Truth."

She smirks. "Of course, you'd take all the fun out of this."

I shrug. I know I'm in trouble no matter how I dice it judging by her devilish grin.

"How do you really feel about Austen?"

"This is stupid. Is there a bathroom around here?" Austen asks before I can answer. She moves to stand, looking around her.

"Don't you want to at least wait until you hear his response?" Aimee mutters.

Aimee's just being nosy and wants to get to the bottom of our past. She likes being in on all the gossip. That and she doesn't like Justin, so any chance she has to drive a wedge between them, she's going to take it.

She won't expect my response, though.

"How do I feel about her?" I repeat her question again, glancing between Aimee and back to Austen.

"She already knows how I feel about her. Don't you Austen?"

There were a few oohs and ahhs from people around us, clearly misunderstanding where this is going.

Austen rolls her eyes, crossing her arms over her chest as if she couldn't be bothered.

"I hate Austen," I say, matter-of-factly.

Austen huffs out a heavy breath, dropping her arms to her side.

"See!" Her gaze shooting daggers at Aimee, motioning to me. "Is this what you wanted to hear? Now, if you'll excuse me, I need to find somewhere to use the restroom."

"I'll take you to the cabin nearby. It's owned by one of the guys in the frat. We can stop there and grab a few drinks," Justin says. His brow raises, and his jaw is set when he looks back at me before following behind her.

"Well, that didn't go quite like I expected," Aimee jokes. She attempts to follow it up with a laugh, but it falls flat.

"Did you seriously mean that?" She turns to look at me.

"Yes," I fire back.

"Whatever," she mumbles under her breath, clearly not believing me. I don't give a shit, though. I'm not trying to prove anything to her.

A few minutes later, Justin comes back with two cups in his hands, one for him and one for Austen.

"You want to explain what that was about?" he questions, puffing his chest out.

I want to tell him to sit down and shut up. If he thinks I'll ever be intimidated by him, he's dead wrong.

"There's nothing to tell."

"You sure about that?"

"Listen, if you want to know something about Austen, take it up with her. I can't promise she'll be truthful with you. She still plays off like she had it rough growing up poor, all while hiding the fact she's loaded. Her dad is a fuckin' millionaire for Christ's sake."

Justin's eyes narrow as if trying to gauge if I'm being truthful.

"I guess what I'm trying to say is don't believe everything you hear and definitely don't fall for the bullshit she feeds you."

He forces an exhale, shaking his head as he stomps back toward the log and takes a seat. Judging by the tension in his body, he's pissed, and I love knowing I'm twisting the knife deeper.

Austen approaches the group then, staring between the two of us. I know it's eating her alive wondering what I said while she was gone.

If she doesn't want me sharing the truth about her past, she should stay away from me like I warned her to.

# Chapter Eleven

## AUSTEN

Sunlight cuts through the blinds, beaming right down on me. I wince at the bright rays, attempting to pull my pillow over my head. The movement causes a jolting pain through my skull, as if it's being split down the middle.

"Oh my God," I groan. I reach my hand out blindly looking for my phone before moving the pillow an inch, enough to peer through squinted eyes.

The time is after noon. How the hell did I manage to sleep so late?

I roll my eyes shut and pull the pillow with me, dropping the phone on the mattress before it bounces onto the floor.

"Why did I drink last night?"

I push myself up and reach for the cord to shut the blinds before leaning back against the wall facing Aimee's bed.

She's gone. If I had to guess, she is either with Darren or off at class. I don't recall anything once I passed out, so I have no idea if she ended up staying here last night.

I had a few beers before asking Justin if we could leave. I was done being around people after the failed game of Truth or Dare.

He didn't seem to mind. Part of me thinks he was excited to get me alone. I could tell he was disappointed when I asked him to take me back to my dorm and again when he tried to kiss me, but I turned him down. I made up some excuse about not being in a good mood.

The truth is, I couldn't stand the thought of kissing him after I had just kissed Ryder earlier that night. Not to mention, there was no part of me that felt the same chemistry with him as I had with Ryder.

What the hell is it about wanting what you can't have that somehow makes it even more tantalizing?

Even Justin knew there was something more between the two of us. He even asked me if that was the reason why.

I force my legs to move across our small dorm toward the mini fridge we keep stocked with cold drinks. I swipe a bottle of water and the ibuprofen off the shelf before quickly downing them both.

Thankfully, today is my day off at the station. I already missed half of my classes, so I decide to email my teachers and apologize for missing today.

There is no way in hell I am going to drag my dead ass anywhere.

I collapse on my bed, tossing my arm over my face, and attempt to fall back asleep, at least until the medicine kicks in and helps alleviate the pounding in my head.

My phone dings as I am drifting off. I absentmindedly reach for it again, remembering how I dropped it on the floor before. I pat my hand on the carpet searching around before I find it, peeking one eye open to read the message.

*Justin: I had a good time last night. We should plan another date again soon.*

There is a part of me that still wants to ask him what was said the night before. Justin's mood had shifted after I came back, and I couldn't shake the lingering questions rolling around in my mind as to why. It wasn't until we left and were alone, he seemed to snap out of it.

I wasn't interested in playing Truth or Dare as soon as Aimee suggested it. We both knew she was using it to dig up dirt on my past with Ryder.

Ryder disappeared for a while before we took off. I half expected him to come back with some no-name blonde on his arm. After his comments about hating me, I knew he was pissed at me for still going on the date with Justin. I couldn't exactly bail on him last minute, especially when he was already outside. Not to mention, I wasn't prepared to answer the endless questions Aimee would throw my way with Ryder standing right there.

I close out of the text message, deciding to hold off until I'm ready to talk to Justin face to face. I push the thought of it out of my mind right now, though, making a mental reminder to text him later to see if he wants to meet up at The Grind.

I lie back down and fall asleep. I'm relieved when I wake up to find the pounding headache has simmered to more of a dull ache. It is bearable, though, which is all that matters.

I manage to pull myself together enough to find a change of clothes and head down the hall for a shower. It feels good standing under the spray, letting the hot water wash over my body.

I opt to spend the rest of the night getting ready for the school week ahead and cap it off with some studying. I order takeout to be delivered and sit down at my desk, ready to crack open my books, when an email comes through.

The subject line is what captures my attention first. "You'll want to read this." It was sent to my personal email, which is my first sign something is off because only my close friends and family have this one.

Curious what it's about, I click on the notification.

*It's not good to be a liar, Austen. The thing about liars is when they come out with the truth, no one tends to believe them.*

*Your secret is safe with me, though, until the time expires.*

I scroll down in the email, my heart dropping when my eyes land on a large image of me. I recognize the picture as the one I took just days before I arrived at Eastwood.

Bile rises in my throat as I continue to scroll, finding several more photos of me in various poses. All of them from my OnlyFun account, some with clothes and others without.

The message ends with a warning that if I don't want to have the photos or my identity shared, I must send $25,000 in Bitcoin with a deadline of two weeks from now.

I slam the lid of my laptop shut, barely in enough time to cover my face as the fountain of tears begin to stream down my face.

Are they kidding? Who the hell thinks I have this kind of money?

More importantly, who would do this to me?

Immediately, Ryder's name flashes through my mind, thinking back to all the cruel and hurtful things he's said since moving to Philly.

It's like the questions swirling around in my head trigger a lightbulb moment, pulling me back to the conversation I had with Mr. Morio about my father.

As if on cue, Aimee comes barreling through the door, tossing two large bags from Neiman Marcus on her bed, kicking off a pair of black patent Louboutin's.

Aimee is the only person who knows anything about my father passing or the inheritance I was set to receive. That's if I didn't decline the money in the meeting set in a week.

Anger simmers under my skin, boiling my blood like hot lava.

I push myself to my feet, storming across the room, and force Aimee against the door. I shove my forearm under her chin, forcing her eyes on me.

"Who the hell do you think you are?" I grit my teeth, spit shooting out of my mouth.

I am angrier with myself for thinking I could possibly trust her, when for so long I've gone on with the thought I can't trust anyone.

I don't want to hurt her, but if anything, I want to send her the warning not to fuck with me. Her eyes bulge out, and her hands fly up. "Holy shit, Austen. What the hell? What is wrong with you?"

"What the hell is wrong with me? I think the question I should be asking is, what the hell is wrong with you? Are you the one behind sending the email?"

"Email? What fucking email are you talking about?"

"Don't play stupid with me."

I search her face, looking for any sign of guilt but come up empty. I push off her and take a step back, shaking my head.

Anxiety rushes through me. Once again, I'm left with no one around me I can trust to lean on. I stalk over to my desk and shove my laptop and chargers into my backpack.

"Where are you going?"

I peer over my shoulder and wince, thinking about how I reacted. She holds up her hands again, shaking her head.

"Don't worry about it," I mutter.

"Listen, I don't know what you think I did, but I can promise you, I had nothing to do with it."

"Did you tell anyone about the inheritance?"

Her brows furrow. She didn't look guilty before, but she sure as hell does now.

"Why? Is that what this is about?"

"Answer the fuckin' question, Aimee."

"No," she sputters. "Of course not."

She's lying. She swallows hard, and I have a feeling it's because she knows I can see through her lies too. The fact she continues to deny it makes me even more pissed off.

I stalk past her toward our closet, shoving a change of clothes into my bag before slipping my phone in my back pocket.

"You don't have to leave. I'll go and stay with Darren for the night. Clearly, you need space."

I brush her off, picking up my backpack and slip it over my shoulder. I step closer to Aimee again, staring her dead in the eye. I want her to see the look on my face and know she heard my warning loud and clear.

"Someone is threatening to leak nude pictures of me if I don't pay them $25,000. If I find out you know who's behind this or you have something to do with it, I want you to hear me when I say I will use every penny of the money my dad left me to bury you. Do you understand me?"

Her eyes flare, and she nods.

Without another word, I storm past her out the door.

I have no idea where I'm going, but I don't care. It can't possibly be any worse than where I've stayed before.

All I know is I want out of here and fast.

# Chapter Nine

## RYDER

"You stupid prick!" Aimee grunts, smacking me in the chest as I walk into her place. "It was you, wasn't it? You're the one behind the email?"

I hold my hands up to block her swings. Darren comes up behind her and wraps his arm around her waist, dragging her away from me.

"What the fuck are you talking about?" I holler. "What email?"

"Who else would it be? Only you and Darren were here when I brought up Austen's inheritance."

"What fuckin' email, Aimee?" I grit my teeth together.

I can tell by the tone of her voice, both equal parts anger and concern, something is going on. Alarm bells go off in my head.

"Austen," she exhales harshly. "I really shouldn't tell you this right now."

"Fuckin' tell me. If she gets pissed, I'll deal with her myself."

She sighs, massaging her fingers over her forehead.

"She got an email. She wouldn't say a lot, so I don't know all the details, but she pushed me against the wall. She practically fuckin' choked me, Ryder, accusing me of being the one behind it before she stormed out of here."

I shake my head. Tension coils in my body. I rub my hand over my jaw, trying to piece together the information I have.

"When was this?"

"Last night. She didn't stay here either. I have no idea where she's at or what's going on. Something's wrong, though. I don't know what, but I'm worried about her."

I pace around the small space of their dorm, trying to piece together the details. She didn't stay long after we played Truth or Dare. She seemed pissed off. Hell, I was too, having to sit there and watch her with Justin when not even an hour before I had my hands roaming over every inch of her body.

"There's more ..." Aimee trails off, staring down at the ground.

"What?" I growl.

"She said they are blackmailing her, threatening to leak nude photos of her if she doesn't pay them $25,000."

My eyes bulge, nearly popping out of my head and rolling across the floor. "Are you fuckin' kidding me?"

She nods, breaking eye contact. She crosses the room and sits on the couch. Me, on the other hand, I'm too wound up and angry.

I'm ready for war.

"You sure it's not your boyfriend over there? He was here too."

"Are you fuckin' kidding me," Darren spits out. His lip curls in a snarl. "You think I give a shit about her? If I want money, I have plenty of ways to get it. I don't need to come after some bitch for it."

"Darren." Aimee stands, putting her body between the two of us.

He holds his hands up and shrugs. "I'm just being honest."

"If you would've kept your fuckin' mouth shut for once, it would've saved us a lot of fuckin' problems that night." I stare at Aimee, gritting my teeth.

"Chill the hell out, all right?"

I stalk away from her, pacing the length of the living room. I need to get out of here. Being cooped up with the two of them isn't helping matters.

"Ryder, I don't think she's going to take the inheritance either. We have no idea who it could be or what they could do if they don't get what they're asking for. That's a lot of money."

Money Austen doesn't have if not for her father.

"If I find out either of you know who it could be or you're keeping anything from me, I'll make you pay for it. You understand me?"

"Dude, you need to chill out. You're comin' for the wrong people here."

I exhale, shaking my head.

"I need you to do me a favor then." I stalk toward Darren. He leans his shoulder against the wall.

He glances away, letting out an exasperated breath. "What, man?"

I curl my lip. "You have connections, people who are smart and can hack into shit. Find someone who can figure out who the hell is behind this."

"You want me to help you hack into some chick's email. The same girl, who just the other night, you were saying you hated?" He chuckles, shaking his head.

He pushes off the wall, turning toward Aimee. "I'm not fuckin' around, Darren." My voice turns low, making it clear I mean business.

The thought alone of someone blackmailing Austen pisses me off, but the fact there are intimate photos of her added to the mix is like pouring gasoline onto a blazing fire.

His body goes tense, and he turns his head back toward me. He narrows his eyes as if waiting for me to magically snap out of a daze.

"You still gonna act like you two don't have history?" Aimee quips.

My gaze darts over to hers. "It's not the sort of history you think we have, all right? Austen and I were in the same foster home growing up. We were like fourteen, maybe fifteen years old at the time. Trust me, it's not what you think. We just get each other, is all."

Aimee nods. I hope it finally sinks in this time, and she'll stop pushing and prodding at the subject, because it's not helping anything either.

"I'll see what I can do," Darren says.

I nod. It's good enough. I won't stop until I get answers. I'm not going to let Austen go through this alone too.

"When I find out who it is, I'm going to bury them six feet under."

"It's like that?" Darren asks, surprised.

"Yeah," I shake my head, full of anger and tension. "It's fuckin' like that."

He sighs and I move to shoulder past him and Aimee. I reach for the doorknob, pausing and turning my attention back to her.

"Text me her number. If you hear from her or if she shows up back here, you will let me know."

"She's already pissed at me enough for getting into her business."

"I'll deal with her, okay? Just do it."

Without another word, I dip out into the hallway and head back to my place. I'm not even out to my car when my phone vibrates in my pocket with a message from Aimee sending me her number. Nothing else.

At least she knows I'm serious.

I send Austen a few messages over the next day or so, all of which go ignored. I'm damn near ready to show up at the police station when Aimee tells me she talked to her and suggests I scope out The Grind.

I shove my phone and keys in my pocket and jog out to my car, heading there in hopes I can run into her.

I take my usual seat in the corner of the coffee shop before she walks through the door. The Austen I remember running into a few weeks ago, the one who was full of piss and vinegar, bouncing her leg to the music, is gone.

She's dressed in her usual dark jeans and shirt, but this time she's wearing a beanie, with the material pulled down past her forehead and a dark pair of sunglasses covering her eyes. It's no secret she's trying to lie low and not draw attention to herself.

Whoever is doing this to her has spooked her enough to go this far.

"Can I get you a coffee?" I ask, coming up behind her.

She jumps, whipping her head around, covering her heart when she realizes it's me.

"Jesus, Ryder. Are you fuckin' following me?" She pulls her sunglasses off.

"Maybe," I say, realizing how bad that sounds. "Sorry, I am, but it's not for the reasons you probably are thinking right now."

I quickly force the words out, not wanting to freak her out anymore.

"Can I get you a coffee, and will you come sit with me?" I nod my head toward the back corner.

Her eyes narrow, no doubt thinking through the questions swirling in her mind. She turns back toward the line before spinning around to face me. "I will, but under one condition."

"What's that?"

"You tell me why you're being so nice."

"I'm not always an asshole, Austen."

She barks out a laugh, earning us a few looks from people around us. She moves her hand to cover her mouth, her cheeks turning rosy.

"You just said 'sorry' to me. When have you ever said that to someone?"

"I can admit when I'm wrong and own up for it."

She's doing her best to stay guarded. It's hard to get a good read on her, but something tells me she's not buying it.

"Buy the fuckin' coffee, Austen, and come sit down."

I take a deep breath and release it slowly as I stalk back toward my spot. She mutters under her

74

breath something that sounds like "told you." I shake my head.

She's once again doing everything she can to drive me crazy.

She grabs her coffee and weaves her way through the tables, back toward the corner where I'm sitting. I have my leg up on the bench beside me, spinning the cup in my fingers, watching her approach.

She pulls out the chair across from me, glancing around the shop before tossing her bag on the empty seat next to her and sits down.

"Cut to the chase, O'Rourke. Tell me what the hell has gotten into you."

"I have a condition myself."

She smirks. "Do tell."

"You don't go flying out of your chair rip-roaring mad like I hear you did with Aimee."

"She told you, didn't she?"

I nod. "She's worried about you. Can you consider the circumstances? Trust me. She started off by laying into me, literally, thinking it was me somehow behind it."

"Are you saying it's not you?" she asks.

I want to be offended she'd think I'd stoop so low, but then again, if I were in her shoes, I don't think there's a person around that I wouldn't wonder had something to do with it too.

"I'm an asshole and a prick, but I would never hurt you this deep."

She releases a shuttered sigh as if all the tension and anxiety coiled inside her is forced right out of her body. She relaxes in her seat and nods, lifting her coffee to her lips, taking a long pull from her drink.

"I guess I'm just questioning everything. I hardly know anyone here, and I'm starting to wonder who I can and can't trust."

She slips her glasses off her face again, along with her hat, setting them on the table beside her. She rakes her fingers through her hair, taming the locks before tucking a strand behind her ear.

She looks beautiful; she always does. It's what makes it so difficult to stay away from her, even five years ago.

I can see in her eyes how much this is wearing her down. She looks like she hasn't slept well. Something about her tossing and turning in her sleep, recalling the first night I stayed with her, makes me angrier.

I clear my throat and her eyes move over, meeting mine.

"Could this be an angry ex-boyfriend or someone from your past? How did someone manage to get their hands on these photos?"

Her throat bobs as she swallows, glancing down at the table. She runs her finger over the edge of her cup, peeling away the sticker on the side.

"I honestly have no idea."

The fact she wouldn't look at me when she said it, the way her voice changed, dropping low, gives me the feeling there is more she isn't telling me.

"Is there anyone other than Justin you've been talking to? Any past boyfriends who could be pissed about you leaving?"

The thoughts running through my head, wondering who it could be, are only making me more and more pissed the longer I sit here.

I keep thinking of her with someone else, their hands roaming every inch of her body the way mine had the night of the bonfire. As much as I want to suspect it could be Justin behind this, it doesn't add up. How could he have access to photos of her in the first place? Don't get me wrong, I'd love a reason to lay my hands on him, but it just isn't adding up.

"No angry ex-boyfriends," she shakes her head. "No one who I'd think would be out for revenge."

"Maybe they're not even angry. It could be someone you think you trust."

"The only person that would fit that description would be you."

My nostrils flare. She presses her elbow to the table, massaging her forehead.

"Austen ..."

"Ryder ..." she counters.

"I know what it feels like to deal with the weight of the world on your shoulders and be left to deal with the fallout by yourself."

I was forced to deal with two parents who left me: one on his own accord and the other who lost her battle to addiction. No one cared enough to take the time to be there for me.

Not until Austen showed up at Haven Brook and sat down at the picnic table. Even staring across the table from her now, it's hard to wrap my head around how we've ended up here. I'm not going to let us go back to the way we were before, though.

She needs me, and damn it, I want to be the one she can turn to.

"You don't have to deal with everything on your own. I get you don't trust me, or anyone, right now. My actions in the past haven't exactly given you the reason to believe you could. I don't blame you either. I promise you, though, I will never hurt you. Not like this."

She glances up, her gaze burning into me as if searching for any sign I could be lying.

"I will prove to you that you can trust me. I'll find out who's behind this. I will not let anyone hurt you."

She looks back down at the table and sighs. "Okay."

I can tell she wants to believe me. I've been in her shoes before. I've heard so many empty promises, you start to expect it won't happen because you know it will inevitably fall through.

I'm going to have to do more than sit here and tell her she can trust me.

I will have to prove it to her, and I will.

Mark my words.

# Chapter Ten

## AUSTEN

It's day three since the email was sent, and my anxiety is at an all-time high.

Last night was the first night I've stayed at my dorm since I got into it with Aimee. I didn't have much in savings, but it was enough to get myself a hotel for a couple of nights. The money is supposed to go toward school expenses. My scholarship is only going to cover so much.

Being alone with these thoughts running through my head is only making it worse.

I'm beginning to overthink all the things that could go wrong if the photos get leaked or word gets out about my OnlyFun page. This has the potential of ruining everything I have worked so hard for.

I could lose my scholarship. I could lose my internship. I'd lose everything I've been working so hard for.

What will happen if I don't give them what they want? What lengths will they go to ruin me?

Aimee texted me a few times here and there, but the truth is, I wasn't ready to talk to her. I learned a long time ago it's best to keep your walls up and not give your trust to anyone. When they inevitably break it, it's easier to pick up the pieces and walk away.

Then, there's Ryder.

It didn't take long for word to travel. I expected it, though. Especially after I slammed his friend against the wall and threatened to hurt her if I found out she had a hand in this.

I'll be honest, it wasn't one of my finer moments.

Ryder has been texting me often since our conversation at the coffee shop. He made it clear he was going to show me I could trust him, and so far, he's following through on his word.

It doesn't mean I'm not waiting for him to be the next person to disappoint me and walk away.

"What do you want now?" I grumble into the phone.

Aimee stayed over with Darren last night. I can't avoid her forever, but I wasn't quite ready for it either.

"Do you have plans today?" Ryder asks.

"Depends ..."

He sighs. "Do you have class?"

Clearly, he isn't going to let this go, so I decide to stop arguing and roll with it.

"I just finished my only class for today. I'm off at the station too."

I don't mention the fact I need to record content for my site, but it can wait. I'm struggling to even do anything where that is concerned, which isn't helping matters.

"Good. I'll be there in a few minutes. Wear comfy shoes and bring a change of clothes."

"Wha-?"

I don't manage to get the word out before the line cuts off and the phone beeps, signaling he ended the call.

"Motherfucker." I grit my teeth and toss my phone on the bed. He said a few minutes, which leaves me with little time to waste. Why the hell do I need a change of clothes, though?

I kick off the boots I wore to class and swap them out for my Vans. I quickly throw my bag on the bed and shove in a pair of jeans, a T-shirt, and a sweatshirt just in case I don't get back until later tonight.

We're rolling into September and the fall weather is around the corner. When the sun starts to set, dipping beneath the clouds, in rolls the chilly air.

I'm zipping up my bag when a text message beeps from Ryder with the word "here."

I want to fire back, demanding he tell me where he's taking me, but I don't. I jog down the stairs and push open the door, stepping into the small courtyard overlooking the parking lot.

I don't see him right away until someone honks from a few spots down. His long, tattooed arm sticks out of the driver's side window, waving me over.

"You couldn't, I don't know, get out of the car and meet me?" I mutter, shaking my head.

This is Ryder we were talking about. Chivalry was dead and gone a long time ago.

The engine of the old Chevy Nova rumbles when he revs the gas and hollers out the window, "Hurry up already, will ya?"

His grin beams through the windshield, and I hold up a middle finger, telling him without words to shove it up his ass.

I toss my bag in the backseat and slide onto the bench seat next to him.

"Where the hell did you get this thing?" I ask, staring in awe at the shiny interior. The smell of leather hits me. The car is in mint condition. If it were possible, I'd have a hard-on from the sight.

I lean forward, running my hand over the dash before breaking my trance to look over at Ryder.

His arm is extended, resting on top of his steering wheel. His muscles flex, looking so effortlessly sexy. He twists a toothpick in his mouth. His gaze trails along my body over to my hand.

"Why haven't I seen this around yet?"

"I don't drive it around campus, because idiots."

I smirk. I can't blame him there. This beauty deserves to be appreciated, and Lord knows what someone would do if they pulled up next to him.

His eyes fall on my mouth and I swear he sucks in a breath before putting the car in reverse, pulling out of the spot. I reach for my seat belt, buckle up, and fold my hands in my lap.

"I'm not telling you, so don't bother asking," he says a few minutes later as we start maneuvering off campus onto the main roads through town.

I turn toward him and narrow my eyes, annoyed he's reading my mind.

"How long am I going to be stuck in here with you then?"

He curves his mouth into a smile, and I roll my eyes, turning my attention out the window to the sights and sounds as we pass by.

We're an hour into the drive when I start getting antsy. Ryder drowns out my incessant questions by turning up the volume on the radio, and I stop asking altogether.

I start to see the signs along the road of an amusement park ahead.

"You're kidding?" I ask, when he veers off, taking the exit.

"What?" He grins and shrugs.

"I've never been anywhere like this before." Tears fill the brims of my eyes, and I quickly blink them away. I glance out the window to avoid Ryder seeing how emotional it's making me.

"I haven't either," he says.

I don't know much about him or his past, outside of our time in Haven Brook, although I suspect we had a lot of similarities in our upbringing.

I still remember overhearing one of the kids mention how his dad skipped out on his mom when he was a baby, and she later died of a drug overdose. Ryder was one of the longest residents there when I arrived, so if anyone knew the abandonment I felt, it was him.

While my mom had an addiction of her own, I was thankful I still had her for as long as I did before she was sent away. Either way, we both had our parents taken from us and were left two broken kids in a very broken system.

Trips to places like amusement parks weren't something I got to enjoy growing up. The fact Ryder thought to get me away from campus and bring me here makes my cold heart melt a little more for him.

We bounce from ride to ride all day, deciding early on to test out every rollercoaster they have. We made a pact not to leave until we hit them all. We don't bother to stop to even eat or play games. I don't remember the last time I laughed or smiled this much.

The sight of Ryder next to me, a grin stretching across his face when we went over a hill on one of the rollercoasters moments before we spun upside down, will forever be ingrained into my memory.

"Oh my God." I giggle, my legs dangling from high in the air. "This is the best day of my life!" I shout into the sky.

Our hands keep finding each other's during each ride. When I look over at him this time and reach for his hand, his gaze shifts and his eyes stare down at my mouth.

I drag my tongue over my lips, wetting them. Even with the loud music playing below, people laughing and shouting in the distance, I can still hear him suck in a breath.

"It's been one of the best days of my life too." He squeezes my fingers in his.

Heat rushes over my body, radiating through my cheeks.

When the ride comes to a stop, I unbuckle the harness and step out of the seat. Ryder reaches for my hand again, slipping his fingers in mine.

"We should get some cotton candy."

I've never tried it before but seeing everyone passing by with cotton candy on a stick makes my mouth water for a taste.

It's getting late, and we still haven't eaten anything of substance. We will need to get something soon. I can't live off water and cotton candy all day. The sky is turning dark, and storm clouds are rolling in. The humidity in the air is thick.

Ryder hands over money to pay for my treat and gives the cotton candy to me. I don't waste any time before diving in, peeling off a piece and shoving it into my mouth.

"Mm," I moan, my eyes rolling closed. "I think I've died and gone to heaven."

My eyes slowly drag open, and I reach for another piece, this one bigger than the last. I stick my tongue out, licking my lips of the sugary sweet taste. My mouth waters the more I eat.

I'm going to get a stomachache, but Lord, it was delicious.

Ryder's two steps ahead of me, staring back at me while I practically drool over my treat. My footsteps slow to a stop.

"Are you sure you don't want some?" I wave my hand at him.

He slowly shakes his head no, watching while I take another bite. His jaw clenches when I suck on the tip of my finger. His eyes turn glossy, his lids lowering with desire.

"C'mere," he grumbles, reaching for my hand.

I could hardly keep up with his long strides, pulling me with him between two buildings until we are out of sight from the crowd of people.

"Is everything okay?" I ask, staring up at him.

He rakes his palms over his face. His movements are jerky and frantic before he drops his hands to his side.

85

"No, I'm not okay."

He takes a step toward me, then another, and another until my back is pressed against the wall. My body trembles against the coolness of the wood.

"Austen," he whispers.

I look around us quickly, checking to make sure we are alone. There are people walking by, laughing and screaming from the rides twisting and turning above us. Yet, right here in this moment, it is only the two of us.

Everything about being with Ryder is a bad idea, but I happen to like bad ideas.

"I want you," he moans, his fingers gripping my hips.

The raspy sound of his voice makes it hard to swallow. I don't think I've ever heard anything so sexy in my life. I don't bother with my cotton candy anymore, dropping it to the ground beside me, wrapping my arms around his neck to pull him closer.

When our lips crash together, it's as if the world around us is crashing too. A bolt of lightning shoots across the sky, and the soft pattering of raindrops fall to the ground around us.

I don't care about anything but tasting Ryder again. I open my mouth, and he drags his tongue over mine, sucking on my lower lip.

"Fuck, you taste sweet," he groans. His words come out breathless as his hand drags over my cheek to cup my face.

The rain starts to pick up, but it doesn't do anything to tamp down the heat burning between us.

He bends down, lifting me into his arms and pinning me against the wall. I lock my heels around him, grinding over his hard length, earning me a low growl.

The awning on the side of the building does little to protect us from the storm, and the rain drenches my hair and my shirt.

"Ryder." My voice cracks.

He pulls back, rain dripping from his brow, gliding down his cheek.

I want so badly for us to go somewhere to be alone, but I'm afraid of what will happen if we stop now.

"Take me to your car," I whisper, pressing another kiss against his lips. "Please."

His thumb brushes over the apple of my cheek, tilting his forehead against mine.

"Let's go."

# Chapter Eleven

## RYDER

Rain pelts against our face as we race through the parking lot toward my car. It was damn near impossible to pull away from Austen when her sweet lips brushed against mine.

The crack of thunder rolling in matches the storm raging in my thoughts. Every second we spent together today was slowly building and building to this moment. We breached the barrier now. The dam is broken, and all I can do now is succumb to it, letting the waves crash over me.

I dash toward the passenger side of my car, shoving the key in the lock and open the door for her. She quickly dives inside just as another bolt of lightning strikes. This one much closer than the one before.

"Ahh, shit," I shout. "Scoot over."

I follow behind her, pushing both of us onto the passenger seat.

Her hair is drenched with strands plastered to her cheek and forehead. She doesn't have a care in the world though, her smile breaks across her face. She lifts her shirt, using the bottom to wipe away moisture from her cheek.

The second my eyes fall on her bare skin, my throat goes dry, causing it to constrict. I exhale harshly, sending me into a coughing fit. I tilt my head back against the headrest, raking my palms over my face, and release a heavy groan.

"Ryder," she says breathlessly. So much heat and desire mixed into one word. I'm ready to beg her to say it again.

"Look at me." Her fingers grip my arm, attempting to peel my hands away from my face.

"I can't."

"You can't?"

"Do you realize how hard you're making this right now?"

"Hard?" she repeats. The subtle croak in her voice made it clear how hard it was for the both of us.

My dick was like a caged animal all day, begging to be set free. The sight of her now, after fighting off this attraction to her for this long, was like tempting a lion with meat. I'm growing ravenous with how much I want her.

The only problem is I don't know if we both want this.

She moves her leg over me, straddling my lap. It's not until she grinds her warm pussy against my dick that my hands finally drop from my face.

"Well, that wasn't as hard as I thought." She quirks her brow, dragging her teeth over her lower lip.

I grip her hips in my hands as she circles her body against me. The move creates a delicious friction causing my dick to strain against the front of my shorts.

"Oh, baby. It's definitely fuckin' hard," I grunt.

She grins this time, grabbing my face in her hands and crashes her lips against mine. The small moan that escapes her mouth has me ready to flip her over and fuck her right on this front seat. She pulls away, arching her back. Her nipples strain against the front of her tank top. I run my thumb over the hard bud, plucking it between my fingers. I push the material over her chest, along with her bra, and suck her pink flesh into my mouth.

She rakes her nails over my scalp, holding me to her. She continues to thrust her hips, riding me through my shorts. She alternates her movements, constantly keeping me guessing.

"You're so fuckin' sexy," I moan, kissing her chest toward her collarbone and up her neck.

She wraps her arms around my shoulders, and I drink in every ounce of her. My fingers run over her back, caressing her soft skin.

I wish we were anywhere but here right now.

Another crack of lightning strikes, followed by a low rumble of thunder in its wake.

"Stay with me tonight," I murmur against her lips.

She pulls back and stares into my eyes, silently asking if I'm sure.

I nod. "We can get something to eat and head back to my place. Stay with me."

She bites down on the corner of her lip, appearing to think about it.

"Why?" As soon as the word is out of her mouth, she seems to second guess it.

"I mean, why do you want me to?"

I don't blame her for wanting to know. The dynamic between us has shifted so quickly, it makes sense she'd suspect I had some ulterior motive.

I still wish she trusted me to talk more about the email and, aside from wanting money, why it seemed to freak her out so much.

What did they have over her?

If she didn't trust me, or my intentions with her, it makes sense why she'd continue to press me further about everything.

"I want to spend time together and fall asleep with you in my arms. Until we get to the bottom of this, I need to know you're safe and protected."

She seems to consider my words, but the reality of the situation hits her when I mention her safety.

The tension in the car shifts, and she climbs off my lap, taking a seat next to me.

We sit there for a few minutes, listening to the soft rain beat against the car.

She rolls her head to the side, staring at me, seemingly lost in thought.

"I'll stay with you," she whispers.

"Good." I smile, climbing over her lap to the driver's seat.

My long legs make it difficult. Some grunting is involved, but I manage to make it happen.

She doesn't move back over to the passenger seat, instead claiming the spot in the middle, resting her head against my shoulder.

I've never been an affectionate person, but something about Austen's touch has me craving more.

We make it halfway back to Philly before we decide to pull off at a small diner along the highway for dinner. The sky is still dark from the storm, but as night starts to fall upon us, we both agree she should probably get something more than cotton candy in her system.

The rain has shifted to a soft mist, although we caught the forecast on the radio saying it's supposed to last all night, as a huge storm is rolling through the east coast.

The diner is quiet, most of the patrons likely heading home for the night.

An older woman with her hair pulled up is standing behind the bar counter, and I motion to one of the booths lining the wall.

"Take your pick," she greets us with a warm smile. "I'll be with you both in just a moment."

Austen leads the way, climbing into the booth, and I slide into the seat across from her. We both pick up the menus and begin browsing through the options.

"So, best day ever, huh?"

She nods. "The best."

She drops the menu onto the table between us and rests her chin on her hand, smiling over at me.

"What was your favorite part?" I ask.

She purses her lips together, thinking about it for a minute. "I loved the Space Shot." She grins.

I smile. We saved the Space Shot for last. It had been my favorite too.

"But ..." she interjects. "I think my favorite was the end of the day. The, uh, cotton candy."

She grins, and warmth covers her cheeks. My eyes fall to her lips. I have the urge to lean over the table and kiss her again.

"I loved the cotton candy too." I wink, and she sighs, shaking her head.

"Can I ask you something?" she asks, her face turning serious.

I have a feeling whatever she's about to ask is going to change things between us. I'm not the greatest about talking or opening up, but if there is anyone who will understand what I've been through, I know it is Austen.

"Shoot."

"Why'd you end up at Haven Brook?"

I sigh and lean back against the booth seat. I've pushed Austen away for so long, but I'm tired of running. From her and from the reality of my past. I look around the room for a second, trying to find the words.

"I was little when my dad left. Real little. Shit, I don't even remember what he looks like. My mom didn't leave any photos behind of him, and his family was never in the picture. He never wanted anything to do with me anyway, I guess, so I didn't bother to look him up."

"I've always had a hard time sleeping. I was awake the night you were brought into Haven Brook, and that's why I knew you were having a bad dream. I could hear you grunting in your sleep from your room."

I release a shuttered breath, staring down at the table. Austen reaches out for my hand.

"We can wait. We don't have to do this now."

"No, it's okay." I squeeze my eyes shut, trying to keep control of my emotions. "I think I need to talk about it."

She nods in understanding. I trace my finger over the back of her hand and continue. "My mom had a lot of guys coming in and out of our place growing up. I can't tell you how many times I've woken up to fighting. They'd be yelling at each other, one thing would lead to another, and I'd find her the next morning with a black eye. One time they hit her so hard, she had a broken tooth. Anyway, I was used to different men coming around. The night my mom died, I remember waking up to one of her many boyfriends trying to crawl in bed with me. Sometimes I swear I can still smell the stench of alcohol on his breath."

She squeezes my hand, attempting to blink away the tears forming in her eyes, sensing where the conversation was going.

"All I remember was him mumbling something about how bad he wanted me." My lip curls in disgust. "One second, I was lying there in my bed, and then the next I was bent over him, my fist pounding into him to the point I couldn't feel anything. I was numb."

"I sat there on the floor staring at his bloody face for a while. He was alive, but he wasn't there, if you know what I mean. Eventually, I got up and went into the living room, trying to find my mom. She was," I exhale heavily. "She was lying on the couch. For a second, I thought she was breathing, but when I bent down close to her, I knew she wasn't."

I pull my hands away from Austen, recalling the sound coming from her throat.

"She overdosed. They couldn't tell me how long she had been gone when I found her, but I still struggle with the fact that if I had gotten up sooner, maybe I could've saved her."

Austen slides out of the booth and takes a seat next to me, wrapping her arm around mine. She leans her head against my shoulder, telling me without words she's here. She's with me.

"I found my mom the same way once," Austen whispers. "She's in prison now, but I know how terrifying that feeling is. I'm sorry, Ryder."

I nod, leaning my head against hers.

The waitress comes around the corner, seeing the two of us sitting together. She nods, flashing us a warm smile before she turns around, leaving us to our moment.

"Thank you for today," Austen whispers.

"Thank you," I repeat back. I think I needed this more than she did.

My phone vibrates in my pocket, and I pull it out to see Darren's name on the screen. I wasn't interested in whatever he wanted to talk about. I suspect he's only calling to see if I'm going to hit up some party with him. I hit ignore before another call comes through again. He must've ended the call and hit redial.

"What?" I bark.

"I knew you were ignoring me," he grunts.

"Why'd you call me back then?"

"Aimee has been trying to get ahold of Austen for the last hour. Is she with you?"

"Yeah, why?"

"Dude, tell her to check her email."

The diner is quiet, and her head is still leaning against my shoulder. She shoots up, reaching over the table to where she left her phone, fumbling it as she tries to type in her passcode. Her hands are shaking, and her face turns white, as if she saw a ghost.

"Aimee," she mutters breathlessly, holding the phone against her ear.

"What is it?" I shout, slamming my fist against the table. I notice a few people turning their heads toward us, along with the waitress standing near the front of the restaurant.

"Are you kidding? Please tell me you're kidding," Austen says, emotion caught in her throat. She rubs her fingers over her forehead and squeezes her eyes shut.

"Will someone tell me what the fuck is going on?"

"Someone sent out a leaked photo. She's naked, man. The face is cut off, but the tattoo. It's Austen."

My jaw clenches, and my nostrils flare. Austen mutters to Aimee she's gotta go, dropping the phone on the table. She buries her face into her palms, sobs racking through her small body.

"I got another email from them, Ryder. They said I'm not taking them serious enough, so now they're demanding $50,000. They threatened to report me to the school. What if I lose my scholarship? My internship? Ryder, I could lose everything if they find out."

I narrow my eyes. "Find out what? It's not like you did this."

She shrugs me off, moving to slide out of the booth.

"Hey, whoa. Where are you going?"

"Can we go? We can pick up something on the way back to your place. I just need to go. I need out of here." She ducks her head, staring around the room. I notice the eyes on us. I can imagine what they're thinking after my outburst.

I nod. I reach into my pocket and toss a twenty on the table. It was the least I could do after coming in here, causing a scene and leaving without even ordering food.

I lead Austen out of the diner and back to my car.

The happiness she wore on her face when we first got here was gone, and I'm pissed at whoever is doing this to her.

# Chapter Twelve

## AUSTEN

Ryder is quiet the rest of the drive back to Philly, leaving me with only the soft sound of the radio playing on low in the background mixed with the rain beating against the windshield.

He tried to get me to talk to him, but in the back of my mind, I'm still struggling to figure out who I can trust.

A feeling deep inside my gut tells me it's not Ryder I need to worry about, even though I can't shake this immense fear I could be wrong.

I zone out along the way, losing track of time. My mind filters through the emails and the photos sent in them. Both pictures had been on my OnlyFun account, which meant whoever it was, knew about my job. Something about succumbing to their threats by deleting my account or handing over the money, money I don't even have, makes me feel as if I am letting them win.

I don't want a penny from my sperm donor, and I refuse to let their threats scare me.

We pull up outside of a large apartment building not too far from campus. Ryder puts his car in park and cuts the ignition, silence falling over us.

He waits for a minute before he tilts his head over to me and asks, "Are you okay?"

The streetlamp in the corner of the parking lot shines enough light for me to make out his features, especially his eyes that smolder like blue crystals. He brushes his thumb over his lower lip, clenching his keys in hand, waiting for my response.

"I don't want to think or talk about it anymore," I whisper. "Today was a great day. It helped me get everything off my mind. Can we keep it that way? Can we not talk about it for tonight and not let it ruin this too?"

I rake my hand through my damp locks, tucking a strand behind my ear. My body hums from the heat of Ryder's stare, burning into me. I tilt my head over to look at him, making out the ridges lining his forehead from his deep scowl.

It's the first time I've seen any real emotion out of him, making me feel like it's bothering him as much as it is me. Normally he's closed off, emotionless, but beneath the dark sky, his walls are coming down.

The rain starts to pick up, and another flash of lightning highlights the sky in the distance, followed by a slow rumble of thunder.

"Let's get inside before it starts pouring again," he says, seemingly agreeing to drop it. He's doing it for me, though, because I can sense the tension rolling off him in waves, wanting answers.

I nod, reaching for the door handle and shove it open just as the rain starts to pick up. The pelts flutter against the ground as we both take off jogging toward the door.

He reaches the door before me, quickly pulling it open, and releases a heavy breath when we enter the enclosed hallway leading to his apartment. The walls are worn down, with various holes patched, along with trash littering the floor. He ducks his head, shoving his hand in his pocket. If he's embarrassed, he has no reason to be. Hell, given all the shit we went through growing up, he should be proud of himself for where he is today. We both should be. We struggled for everything we had and here we are, fighting tooth and nail to overcome the shitty life we were dealt.

He unlocks the door to his apartment, pausing to turn toward me, his back against the door.

"You're the first person I've ever brought here," he murmurs.

His eyes appear to lose focus, staring behind me for a brief moment, lost in thought. When they lock back on mine, something in them shifts. I can't quite explain it, but I have a feeling whatever happens tonight between us, there will be no going back to who we were before.

"I've never stayed over with someone before," I say, realizing how stupid it sounds coming out of my mouth. "I mean, not like this. I've stayed over with family and at countless foster homes, but never someone that I ... where there was. You know."

A small smile curves the edge of his mouth, saving me from rambling any further.

He reaches for my hand and pushes the door open, leading me inside. The callouses on his fingers brush over my skin, and all I can think about is how they'd feel on every sensitive part of my body. He slams the door behind me, pinning my back against the wall. The light from outside casts a soft glow through a large window on the opposite side of the room; otherwise, we're cloaked in darkness.

He takes a step toward me, and I tilt my head against the wall, releasing a shuttered breath. He lets go of my hand, sliding his fingers over my forearm, moving to grip my hips. I hold on to him, tilting my head back until my eyes fall on him.

He leans in and runs his nose over the column of my neck. His warm breath skates along my skin. I tremble, triggering each of my senses.

I'm consumed.

When he brushes his lips along my neck, I let out a throaty moan and dig my fingers into his arm.

"Ryder," I breathe.

"Mmhm," he hums.

"You should know …" my voice shutters. "I've never been with anyone before."

I wanted to follow it up with "not like this," but I am not ready to tell him about the life I keep hidden.

I need him to understand the gravity of what this means to me.

When I first showed up at Haven Brook, something about him spoke to me. I sought out comfort in him, and at first, he welcomed it. He opened up to me, but as soon as his walls started to come down, he was quick to force me away, and the walls went right back up.

I didn't want the past to repeat itself again, especially after tonight.

"I don't want to hurt you," he whispers, pressing his forehead against mine. "I never did, even back then."

He pulls back an inch, tracing his finger along my jaw before pressing his mouth against mine. The kiss starts out firm, but as my body relaxes so does his, and our lips soften against each other.

I slip my arms around his shoulders, which isn't easy to do with our height difference.

He breaks the kiss, his eyes staring into mine. His tongue drags across his lips. The sight has desire pooling low in my belly.

"I won't let anyone else hurt you either." The words spoken with conviction but with an edge of pain too. "I don't know what they have over you or how they got those pictures of you. Just know," he pauses, "I won't let you fight this battle alone. I'll go to war with anyone who tries to hurt you."

"Ryder," I murmur, reaching out to tangle my fingers with his. The move seems to relax him again, letting go of whatever thoughts or fears were rolling through his mind.

"I want you ..." I pull him closer to me again.

He takes a step between my legs and reaches down, gripping my thighs as he lifts me into his arms. I circle my legs around him, molding my body against his.

I kiss up the curve of his neck, and he turns to carry me through the dark apartment, down the short hallway. He kicks the door open. Out of the corner of my eye, I spot his bed near the corner of the room.

It's massive, much bigger than the one I'm used to sleeping in back in my dorm, but it makes sense considering he stands nearly a foot taller than me.

He carries me over and playfully drops me on the edge of the bed, sending me falling backward against the mattress. I laugh, tilting my head back arching my back toward him. I watch as he stares at me with rapt attention.

He bends down on the floor, unties my shoes, and tosses them near the closet behind him.

I drag my lip between my teeth, staring down at him. My mind flashes back to the Ryder I saw with Big Boobs McGee, recalling how he gripped her hair in his fist.

Something about this sweet side feels all wrong with Ryder.

"What?" he stares up at me, his fingers massaging the bottom of my foot.

I grin. "I guess I didn't picture you being so ... sweet."

He tosses his head back and laughs. The sight of his throat and the subtle bob of his Adam's apple had me clenching my thighs together.

His gaze falls on my legs before meeting mine again.

"I guess I thought for the first time I'd take it slow."

"The first time?" I question. He was already thinking about the next time.

He smiles and nods. "It's not even ten o'clock yet, Austen. A whole lot of night is still left."

I swallow hard at the thought.

His fingers brush over my ankle and up my leg. Each pass his hands make over my skin toward my thighs, I can feel my body relaxing more. When his fingers graze the hem of my shorts, he moves my leg over his shoulder and kisses a trail following the same path his hands made.

"Lie back," he urges, and I fall back to my elbows.

He rolls his eyes and shakes his head, not surprised by the fact I don't take directions from him. His hand runs over the front of my shorts, pausing to press against the seam between my legs. I suck in a deep breath at the sensations spreading through my body.

I've never been shy about exploring my body, but the way my body reacts to his touch is different than anything I've felt before. In my mind, when I share pictures of myself on the internet, I am doing it under the guise of Violet. No one knows it's me, so there is a safety net in knowing my identity is protected in a way.

Even when I had moments of doubt, I always told myself it was a job.

A means to an end.

It also helped build confidence in myself I had lost somewhere along the way. As much as I hate to feel like I put my worth into how strangers online saw me, it felt good to feel wanted by someone for once.

This, with Ryder, is different, though.

The way he looks at me, the race of adrenaline shooting through me every time he kisses me, the need I feel wanting him to touch every inch of my body.

I want more of him in every way.

I listen to his ask and finally drop to the bed. He reaches for the button of my shorts, undoing it before sliding them down my legs.

"Fuck," he mutters under his breath, and I grin at how unrestrained he sounds.

He brushes his lips over the apex of my thigh, this time following the path until he brushes his nose through my folds. He takes a deep breath and I slap my hand over my mouth.

Any mortification I felt at the thought of him smelling me is forced out of my mind when he sucks my clit through my underwear. I thrust my hips toward him. The move has him growling under his breath.

He pulls back, reaching for my panties, and slips them down my legs. He holds them up, waiting until I'm watching him before pressing them against his face, inhaling them.

"Ryder," I chastise, my mouth dropping open.

"You smell so fucking good."

I fling my arm over my face, unable to believe what I just saw. His fingers trace over my folds. My stomach quivers at the feel of him touching me.

When he brushes over my clit, I roll my eyes back and let my legs fall the rest of the way open.

"Tell me how bad you want me," he moans, tracing his finger over my opening.

I'm unable to form a word, lost in the sensation spreading through my body. He's barely touching me, and yet I feel like I'm on the brink of going insane. I don't know if I want to beg him to touch me or reach my hand down to do it myself.

Each pass his fingers make up and over my clit and back down only to push just the tip of his finger into my center has me ready to beg him to stop talking and give me what I want already.

"Please," I moan. It's all I'm able to force out.

"Please, what?"

"I'm not kidding."

"Neither am I," he says, pulling his hand back from me.

I push myself back up to my elbows, staring down at him. He raises his brow, challenging me. I narrow my eyes, moving my hand over my stomach down between my legs.

His gaze burns into me. For a second, I almost think he's surprised by my bold move before he pushes my hand out of the way and I playfully swat back at him.

He moves to stand, climbing over me.

"Stop." He grits his teeth, and I smile back at him.

"Are you trying to push my fucking buttons, Austen?"

I shrug. "Maybe."

He clenches his jaw. I continue to rub my clit, but I tune him out, closing my eyes and letting my mouth drop open to release a moan.

"Get up on the bed, Austen," he says. He waits for a second for me to stop and crawl up his bed. When I don't move, he follows it up with, "Now."

"Always so damn moody."

He lets out a slow chuckle, but not one that finds what I said humorous, more as if to say, "you have no fuckin' idea." I give in and crawl up the mattress, falling back against his pillows.

He stands at the end of the bed, ripping his shirt over his head. My eyes soak in the sight of his naked body on display for me, along with the Zeus tattoo spanning the front of his chest blending into the one covering his arm.

He reaches for the waistband of his shorts, pushing them down and kicking them off. My eyes damn near pop out of my head at the sight of his length bobbing at attention.

"If you keep staring at me like that, I'm going to find something to go into that mouth of yours."

His nostrils flare when I follow it up by tracing my tongue over my lip.

"I'm going to get you back for this. You just wait."

"I'm waiting," I fire back.

He crawls up the bed toward me, his eyes blazing into me as he does. I move my legs open for him, challenging him the closer he gets.

He reaches for my ankle, pulling me toward him. The move sends me to my back before he pushes my legs against my chest, taking the wind right out of me.

"Hold your legs up." His voice is firm, commanding.

He lifts my ass in the air before he bends down and traces a path from my pussy to my clit. I'm unable to move with the weight of my body nearly folded in half.

All I know is I don't want him to stop. I never want him to fucking stop.

When he sucks on my clit, I can barely understand the words coming out of my mouth. I know they can't possibly make any sense though, most of them unintelligible sounds more than anything.

He dips his finger back into my pussy, and this time he gives me more than just the tip. Judging alone by the size of his finger, I can't imagine what it will do when he slips inside me for the first time.

"It's going to feel so fuckin' good."

He responds, and I realize I must've voiced my thoughts out loud.

Before I have a chance to overthink it, he lowers me back down to the bed and moves until he's positioned above me, brushing the head of his dick through my folds. I wrap my legs around his waist, attempting to pull him closer to me.

He leans over on his forearms, pressing a kiss against my lips. When he slowly enters me, he breaks the kiss, pushing his forehead against mine while we both struggle to get a hold of ourselves.

Once he's all the way inside me, he rolls his eyes shut and lets out a heavy puff of air. When his eyes find mine, he reaches his hand up, his thumb caressing the apple of my cheek.

"Are you okay?" he whispers low.

I'm unable to speak, so I respond with a subtle nod before I wrap my arms around his neck, pulling him back down to kiss me again.

This time when he does, he thrusts his hips back before they piston toward me.

Each push of his hips drives me further and further to the edge until we're both standing right there on the brink together. When he leans back, he reaches his hand between us and rubs his thumb over my clit. I release a loud moan, clawing at his arms, begging for more.

I'll never forget the sound of Ryder groaning my name when I fell over the edge.

I'm in deep with him now. So deep I hope I never have to come up for air.

# Chapter Thirteen

## AUSTEN

I drag my ass out of Ryder's bed the next morning and force myself to shower before heading to class. I'm amazed I'm able to focus on anything but our night together.

Every inch of my body hums at the thought of his touch, remembering the way his hands gripped my hips, the memory of his fingers slipping inside me, his mouth licking and sucking while he did.

The thought alone sends my body breaking out in shivers, and it has nothing to do with being cold.

I'm ready for a nap when I make it back to my dorm, opening the door to find Aimee sitting on her bed.

I stop in my tracks, staring at her. She doesn't look like her usual self. She's dressed down in a pair of cotton shorts and a T-shirt. Her makeup is removed, and her hair looks frizzy like she hasn't yet styled it for the day. Hell, even her usual smile stretched across her face is gone.

"Hey," she whispers, flashing me a wave.

I nod, tossing my bag on the floor and kicking off my shoes.

I know we need to talk about what happened the last time the two of us saw each other. Part of me is avoiding the conversation altogether. We haven't spoken much, aside from the phone call at the diner and a few text messages. I'm not sure I'm ready to face the reality of my actions.

"I was hoping we could talk," she says.

I exhale and turn back to look at her. She crosses her legs beneath her and folds her hands in her lap. She looks as uncomfortable as I feel, but something about it breaks the ice.

"I think it's time," I agree, climbing onto my bed, facing her.

"I want to start off by apologizing. I've gotten into your business a few times since we met. It was never with the intention of hurting you, though. All I did was mention to Ryder in front of Darren how your dad passed away and left you an inheritance. I didn't give him any of the details, other than how you want nothing to do with it."

"Is that the only time it was ever brought up?"

She nods before she suddenly stops. Her eyes flashing in realization.

"What?" I bark.

She holds her hand up. "Ryder made a comment the night of the bonfire when you went to the cabin. He called you fake and told Justin to be careful. Something about how you liked to pretend you had it rough growing up, but it's a lie. He told him your dad was a millionaire."

My heart starts to pound, and I push myself off the bed, pacing the length of the room.

Immediately, my mind goes to Justin, suspecting it could be him.

Why would it be him? Not only does he have plenty of his own money, he has always treated me well when we've been together. Even when I turned him down after he tried to kiss me, he was a gentleman about it.

The entire drive home, he was sweet and made small talk about how much the old pickup he was driving meant to him. I was surprised it still ran, but he told me the story about how it was his dad's first truck, passed down to him from his grandpa, and how his dad did the same when he turned sixteen.

We've exchanged a few texts since. He seemed to catch on to the fact I'm not interested in him.

It still didn't add up how he'd get the pictures, though. As soon as the thought crosses my mind, I already cross him off the list of possibilities. If Ryder said something at the bonfire, it could be any number of people who may have overheard.

"I don't think Ryder meant to hurt you, Austen." Aimee winces, biting her lip.

"It's okay. I don't think he intended for this all to happen either."

"I thought it was all harmless fun, me trying to push the two of you together. I saw the connection between you two the very first day we met. Ryder has never shown interest in a woman, except maybe when he was looking to hookup at a party. He's tried to play it off like it was in my head, but we all know there's more between you two."

I rub my lips together. Aimee doesn't even know the right turn our relationship took after we spent yesterday together.

"I guess I thought I was doing the two of you a favor. You're both stubborn. I wanted to play matchmaker and get you to see what's right in front of you."

"We did know each other from back home, but I'll give you some credit."

Her eyes light up. "Darren said you were together last night when he called Ryder about the photos. Did you ...? Are you saying you're ...?"

She pushes herself off the bed, bounding to her feet. She claps her hands together with excitement, and I laugh.

I nod. "I stayed over with him last night."

Her mouth drops open, and her eyes bug out. "You're kidding me."

I shake my head, smiling.

"Holy shit." Her face is one of shock, her jaw practically unhinged. "I don't think Ryder has ever taken a woman back to his place before."

I chuckle. "He hasn't. He made it a point to tell me last night actually."

She sits on the edge of her bed, bending over with her hands on her knees. "You have to tell me about it. Was it good? Is he big? He has to be. You know what they say about those tall, lean guys. His hands are massive, and he has big feet. All signs say he's packin' heat."

She winks; her mouth rattles off a mile a minute. I throw my head back, trying not to laugh, but I can't help it.

"You're not going to tell me, are you?" She deflates.

My mind flashes to what he'd say or do if he found out I told Aimee what went down between us. "All I will say is it was good ... very good. More than good." I smile.

"You're blushing." She wiggles her finger, pointing it toward my face. "You lucky bitch."

She pushes to stand and stalks across the room toward the closet. She opens the door, staring at her reflection in the mirror before turning back to face me. She rummages through her pile of makeup before dabbing foundation on her face.

"I'm sorry for putting my hands on you like I did."

She stares at me, her hand held in the air waiting for me to continue.

"No excuses, Aimee. I just got so mad and, I guess I thought you had something to do with it. I didn't know anyone here. I mean, I knew Ryder, but I never thought I could trust him. I thought I'd have everything, my scholarship, my internship taken away from me."

"You scared the hell out of me." She laughs, going back to doing her makeup. "I won't lie, I thought you were going to kick my ass right there, but you didn't hurt me. You made your point."

"I'm sorry though, it won't happen again."

"Damn straight, it won't." She fires back. "I'll be ready next time, and I'll kick your ass too."

I know there is an edge of seriousness to her tone, but I shrug it off. We both said our piece, and now we're brushing it under the rug.

"Be honest with me, and I swear I won't open my mouth this time. How do you think someone got their hands on those pictures?"

I swallow hard, avoiding her burning gaze. This isn't something I've told anyone. It's not because I'm ashamed or embarrassed, although I do get mortified at the thought of someone close to me seeing my content.

I exhale slowly, not sure how to explain it to her.

"They were calling you Violet Grace online. Is that like an alias or something?"

I nod. She gives me a couple minutes, attempting to sort through how to explain this to her.

"Have you heard of OnlyFun?"

"Girl, are you kidding me? Who hasn't?" She laughs. "Is that where those photos are from?"

I nod again, fidgeting my hands in my lap.

"Quit the shy act. You can't tell me you took those pictures and then start acting like this now. I bet you're wild in bed." She cackles. "No wonder Ryder wants you. I've heard he's into that rough sex. Will you two let me watch?"

My eyes bulge out of my head as the dorm room door swings open. Ryder always has a way of picking the perfect time to walk through the door, choosing this moment to show up.

"What's up?" he asks as Darren steps in behind him. Ryder disregards everyone else in the room and stalks over toward me, tipping my chin up like he's going to lean over and kiss me.

He realizes then he's walked in on something. Aimee's too focused on him touching me to even form any words.

"Did I interrupt?" He looks from me over to Aimee. Darren acts like he doesn't want to be here, claiming his usual spot leaning against the wall.

"You going to act like," she points her makeup brush at where his thumb is still pressed beneath my chin, "*this* whole thing isn't happening now? I'm not an idiot. You two can stop the whole act now."

Ryder turns his gaze back toward me. We hadn't really talked about what happens now, but I also hadn't expected him to walk in here and act the way he is either.

She would know something was off now.

He drops his hand to his side and takes a seat across at Aimee's desk.

"You gonna ignore me?" She spins around.

Ryder shrugs, not bothering to elaborate.

"To answer your question, Ryder, you did interrupt. I was in the middle of asking her if she'd let me watch you two together. I can only imagine how wild you both are."

He chokes on air, sending him into a coughing fit. I can't control myself either, spiraling into a fit of laughter.

"You told her?" he mouths to me.

"She figured it out herself," I mutter.

"I told you I'm not an idiot, Irish. You'd do well to remember that too," Aimee snaps back.

Ryder shrugs, pushing himself to his feet. He takes the two steps separating us and tilts my head up toward him again. When he leans over and presses a kiss against my mouth, the room goes quiet. I'm not sure if it's because I'm drowning everything out or if they're as speechless as I am. When he pulls back, he flashes me a wink and takes a seat again.

"Jesus," Aimee whispers breathlessly.

I bite down on my lip, fidgeting again. I'm thankful when my phone vibrates in my hand with a text message coming through, giving me a distraction from how badly I wish we were alone.

**Aimee: I promise I won't tell him or anyone anything.**

Another message comes through.

**Aimee: I was serious about watching too.**

She follows it up with a devil smiling emoji, and I close out of the message, shaking my head at her from where she's staring at me from her reflection in the mirror.

She may have heard about Ryder liking it rough in the bedroom, but what she hasn't heard about me is I don't do well with sharing.

Ever.

# Chapter Fourteen

## AUSTEN

When Monday rolls around, I'm not ready for what I have to do.

I didn't tell Ryder about the meeting with the lawyer. It wasn't my intention to keep it a secret, but I wasn't ready to talk about it either.

I am still dead set on not accepting the money. Something about taking it, or hell, even letting the person behind the emails get to me, feels like I am letting them win.

My dad chose a long time ago to have nothing to do with me. The only reason he ever came around, when he rarely did, was because of his ongoing affair with my mom.

I hated him for what he did to her.

While I know she's accountable for her own actions, even the ones that inevitably led her to prison, I know he was the one who used and enabled her. All he cared about was sex, using her for his own twisted needs.

When he was done and got what he wanted, he threw money at her and walked away.

I can't help but feel like this is what he was doing with me too.

He knew she wasn't in any place to care for me either. Did he worry about where the money was going or even about my health and wellbeing? Nope. He was feeding his own addiction, and subsequently, my mom's as well.

I am collateral damage in it all.

Now I look at where she is and remember how he refused to give her the help she needed, especially when he had the means to do so. It only makes me hate him more.

He was a coward, and I refuse to live my life being a coward too.

The bus ride to Cleveland is about two hours long. I've been making a new playlist of songs I've been listening to lately, so I put in my headphones and drown out the world, helping the time fly by quicker.

I have about thirty minutes left to kill before my meeting with Mr. Morio. I decide to go for a walk nearby, attempting to clear my head and calm my nerves. I know there is a chance I'll have to face his other family. I keep picturing the look on their face when I walk in, the product of his infidelity.

His dirty little secret.

The child he never wanted to have but was stuck with.

I want to get this over with already.

My phone vibrates in my pocket as I take a seat along the park bench. I pull it out as another message from Justin flashes across the screen. We've spoken a few times over the past couple weeks. I told him I wasn't interested in dating right now, making up the excuse I had a lot on my plate with school and family stuff.

It's all an excuse, though, even I know it as I sit here and stare at his message. It doesn't bother me in the slightest adding Ryder into the mix. I'll make time for him over everything.

That realization speaks volumes to me.

Justin is being nice, though, asking how my weekend went. I don't want it to lead into him asking me to get together because, honestly, I was hoping he'd get the hint already.

I swipe the message on my screen, deleting it before locking my phone. The time flashes on my screen. I've wasted every minute I had.

It's time to get this over with.

Dread fills the pit of my stomach. I wish more than anything I could hightail it back to the bus station and not go through this period. Yet still, I feel like I'm giving in, and I'm not going to let anyone force me to cower in the corner anymore.

It's been years since I last saw my father, yet I can still picture his face vividly in my mind. My mom had told me about his wife and their children. The urge to look them up online was there. All it would take is one quick Google search. It wouldn't be hard to find Robert Roseto, along with all the information out there on his family.

Yet, I never did.

Still, I don't think any of the information or ammunition would've prepared me for the moment when I see them sitting in front of me.

An older woman is sitting at the end of the long, oak office table. She's wearing a dress suit with pearls around her neck. Her hair is fixed neatly, every strand perfectly in place.

Next to her are two raven-haired men, who remind me of the photos I've seen of my father growing up. They are tall, demure, and both dressed in a suit and tie. It feels like I am walking into a boardroom meeting with Cleveland's finest.

Meanwhile, I'm wearing my nicest pair of black denim jeans and sneakers, topped with my short-sleeve gray Henley.

I'm the odd one out, but it's comfortable, given it has been my wardrobe for most of my life.

"Hello, you must be Austen." The older woman greets me with a warm smile. Something about her soft voice breaking through the silence feels strangely calming.

I nod.

"I'm Lillian Roseto, and these are my two sons, Philip and Michael."

They both return their mother's smile, and I can't help but notice the similarities in their features when they do. For a moment, I wonder what they think of me sitting on the other side of this table, but I force the thoughts out of my mind.

I don't care what they think of me. As far as I'm concerned, once I walk out of this office, I'm never going to see or speak to them again.

I duck my head down, rounding the table, and take a seat across from them as Mr. Morio walks into the room. He takes a seat at the head of the table with two large envelopes in his hand.

"Shall we get started?" he asks.

We all nod, and we do.

I've replayed how this would go in my head at least a hundred times since the day I got the phone call. What I expected to happen when I walked in here, is in fact, the exact opposite.

"Before we get started on discussing the estate, I want to thank you for coming today, Austen," Lillian says. "I want you to know none of us at this table would blame you if you chose not to come. I didn't know about you or your mother until you were much older. Even then, your father was adamant about not reaching out to you. I didn't know your mother was in prison until Mr. Morio tried to contact you about being here today. I want you to know everyone at this table today believes you are just as entitled to his estate as we are. In fact, I'd argue in many ways you deserve this more. As you'll find listening to the settlement agreement, we felt it was only right we make up for what you've missed out on growing up."

My brows furrow, and I turn to Mr. Morio. "What does that mean exactly?"

"Well, you see, your father wrote in his will that he would leave the residence and a large sum of money to Mrs. Roseto. He's passing down Roseto Enterprise to his two sons, who will take over his businesses. The rest of his money will be left to you."

I don't know how to respond. Hell, I can hardly swallow through the ball of cotton forming in my throat.

"Okay ..." I trail off.

"This will leave you with an estimated two-point-three million dollars before taxes. A portion of this will go to your school. I understand you're a student at Eastwood University. We will remit payment for your tuition and any expenses pertaining to your room and board while you're enrolled, along with an allowance to help cover personal expenses while you focus on your studies. After you graduate, the rest of the money will be paid to a trust, and you'll have access to this when you turn twenty-five years old."

I sag against my chair, staring from Mr. Morio to Lillian sitting across the table. She moves to stand, reaching across the table to clutch my hand, squeezing it in hers.

"Please take this. You deserve it."

There is something so motherly in her tone. I expected to walk in here and find someone cold and distant, feeling greedy after learning about her husband's affair, wanting to keep every penny for themselves. I was prepared to tell them to take it and shove it up their ass.

The warm smile on her face and the softness in her voice makes me feel as though she wants this for me more than I do. There isn't an ounce of pity on her face or in her words, only someone who is looking out for me, the same I'd suspect she would for her own children given the circumstances.

They aren't the vile and heartless people I thought I'd meet today.

None of us are. If anything, we were all innocent bystanders in the destruction my father brought to everyone around him. He had shown time and time again how selfish he was, not only in how he treated me and my mother, but even how he regarded the people sitting across from me.

Somehow, he managed to find the one woman who was the opposite of him in every way, and she was collateral damage in this too.

When I walk out of the office, I am still undecided as to whether I'll accept the money or not, but I feel the noticeable weight lifted off my shoulders when I leave. Mr. Morio told me he'd give me time and asked me to be in touch with him in the next few days.

I'm ready to break out of here in a sprint toward the bus station, wanting to get back to Eastwood. When I jog down the front steps, I pause when I see the black muscle car parked outside with Ryder leaning against the passenger door.

His arms are crossed over his chest, the sleeves of his black T-shirt tightening around his muscles.

"How'd it go?" he asks, pushing off the car before walking toward me.

"Better than I expected."

His eyes brighten at my response. I know he wants to know more, but I'm not ready to talk about it. I need to wrap my head around everything myself first.

"What are you doing here?"

"Well, you hadn't been responding to my text messages today, so when I stopped over at your dorm to find you gone, I got worried."

He chuckles, running his hand over his jaw. "Worried, huh?"

"Yeah, I may have caused a bit of a scene until Aimee agreed to tell me where you were. She wants to make it known if you're mad at her for telling me, she's going to beat my ass."

I throw my head back and laugh. The tension between Aimee and I is lifting, and I'm beginning to warm up to her again. I'm being cautious, still not sure who I can trust these days.

"Well, you found me."

"She told me the name of the lawyer and what time you had your meeting. I may have hightailed it here. I thought you could use the moral support. If anything, you could use me as a ride back to Philly."

He glances around as if expecting someone would notice him.

"What, you don't want to stick around here?"

"Hell no," he quips. "Can we get out of here already? I'll take you back to my place. Make you dinner. Whatever you want."

"You drive a hard bargain," I joke.

"You drive me crazy. Get in the damn car."

He reaches for the handle, opening the door for me, and tilts his head over, signaling for me to get in already.

"Always so bossy," I joke as he grunts and shuts the door behind me.

# Chapter Fifteen

## RYDER

"You need to relax, man!" Darren grunts, smacking me on the chest.

"You mean to tell me if someone was doing shit like this to Aimee, you wouldn't be reacting the same way?"

He pulls up outside the rundown warehouse. On the outside, you wouldn't expect it to be someone's house, but I've heard about some of the shit Reza has done for Darren over the past couple years. I'm not surprised he's living here, and I'm willing to bet he has this place locked up like a fortress.

He puts his BMW in park and turns the key in the ignition. "Oh, it's like that now, is it?"

I shrug him off, pushing my door open and slamming it shut behind me.

"You gonna answer me or not?" he asks when he realizes I'm blowing him off. I don't have the patience for his shit right now.

"Was there a question?"

"You care to elaborate why this girl has you all riled up? Last I heard, you were announcing to half of Eastwood how you hated her. Now you're out here trying to take down any person who's wronged her."

"It's not any of your business …" I say, kicking the gravel on the ground, approaching the large metal door.

We see a keypad near the door with a large security camera overhead. Before we have a chance to ring the bell, a voice comes over and says he'll be right out.

"Jesus," I mutter under my breath.

Darren chuckles, seemingly understanding our conversation is over.

A few seconds later, Reza sticks his head outside. I've seen him a couple of times, he's been to some of the fights at The Ring. He's about a foot shorter than me but built like a brick shithouse.

He's the type you don't want to underestimate because one second you think he's on your good side, and the next he'll take you by surprise.

"What's up, man?" Darren asks.

I follow behind them into the large industrial building. One side is built like a condominium, with a large garage down below. The space is open with a kitchen and living area. Two bedrooms are along the back wall facing Meadow Lake.

He waves over his shoulder for us to follow him. My eyes take in the warehouse. If I were to buy my own place one day, I'd love to have something like this.

I grew up living with small bedrooms, often sharing a room with three, sometimes even four, other kids. The thought of having this much space, cut off from the rest of the world, sounds perfect.

Reza stands near the doorway, staring back at me, seemingly waiting for me to pick up the pace.

He leads us into a large computer room with six different computer screens stacked two at a time in a half-circle facing his desk. He pulls out his chair and takes a seat, turning to look at me.

"Darren said you wanted me to dig into an email that was sent to a friend of yours. Something about her being blackmailed."

I nod. "Someone sent her an email over a week ago threatening her, wanting some money. The email came shortly after she found out her dad passed away, leaving her with a sizeable inheritance."

"Does she know you're doing this right now?"

I shake my head. "She keeps blowing it off, saying she's not going to let them get to her. The thing is, this person is amping things up now. Over the weekend, a mass email was sent out to several students with an explicit photo of her. Her face isn't shown, but anyone who knows her will recognize it's her."

"Can I see the picture?" Reza asks.

My face drops. "Excuse me?" I grit my teeth.

He chuckles. "Not for that reason," he laughs again, running his hand over his face. "I may be able to trace the source of the message. Can I see it?"

I huff out a breath and I can sense Darren's eyes on me. Thinking back on our earlier conversation when we arrived, I practically hear the questions burning in his mind.

I pull out my phone and notice a message from Austen. I close out of the notification, scrolling to the email and hand it over to him.

He lets out a slow whistle, wiggling his brows. I take a step toward him before Darren moves between us and Reza lets out a loud throaty laugh. He holds up his hand and smacks his leg.

"Dude, chill, man. She's working with the wrong kind of equipment, but even I can appreciate a beautiful woman."

I drop my hands and turn away from him, running my hand over my scalp. My shaved head feels like rough sandpaper along my skin, but it helps distract me from the moment.

He turns back toward his computer and the keys start clicking away as he's typing, pulling up various screens. A few minutes later he asks me a question about what email she's using and for her full name before the keys resume typing away.

I can't possibly keep up with what he's doing, so I turn my back to him, needing a moment to myself.

"Does she go by the name Violet?"

"Huh?"

I turn to face the screens again and he has what appears to be an email inbox popped open on the screen. I catch a glimpse of the subject line.

"I see emails addressed to someone by the name of Violet Grace. It's likely an alias, though, because most of these are coming from an OnlyFun account."

"OnlyFun? What the hell is OnlyFun?"

Reza clears his throat and glances over at Darren who's standing stoically in the corner. His arm is crossed in front of him, brushing his thumb over his lower lip.

"It looks like this email is set up as the account holder. I can try to get into her OnlyFun site if you want me to, but I just want you to be prepared for what you might find."

"What the fuck is OnlyFun?"

"It's a website people use to share online content with a list of subscribers."

"Okay ..." my voice trails off. "What's the big deal exactly?"

"It's explicit online content."

A storm of questions crashes down around me. Explicit content?

Does this mean she's using this website to sell photos like the one in the email? Why would she do that?

"The person who sent the emails is likely someone who is subscribed to her OnlyFun account and is using this as leverage over her."

"Do it."

Darren holds his hand out to stop me. "Man, I don't know if you want to go down this road. Maybe you should talk to her first."

"If the person is likely on her subscriber list, can you try to figure out who it is from her account?" I ask.

He exhales harshly and nods, turning back toward his computer. His fingers resume flying over the keyboard, typing away. Meanwhile, I'm left pacing back and forth in this small room.

It's something I used to do growing up. Anger often gets the best of me, but I find it helpful if I focus on counting my steps from one side of the room to the other.

I got in too much trouble as a kid, and I needed a way to channel my aggression before I ended up flipping tables and taking it out on the wrong person.

"All right, I'm in."

I squeeze my eyes shut and release a deep breath before I turn back to the screen. Immediately my eyes are met with a picture of Austen. She's dressed in what looks like a black one-piece swimsuit, but judging by the lace covering her body, it looks more like lingerie.

He continues to scroll through various images, landing on one she posted the night of the bonfire. It was right before I showed up at her dorm. Each of the photos and videos are from her neck down.

To anyone else, they wouldn't know who she was except for her wildflowers tattoo on her forearm, which gives it all away.

I know it's her. The emotions hitting me range from desire in seeing her in all these different photos to anger at the thought of anyone else seeing her this way.

I want to ask her why, but in the end, I know why.

Despite what I said the night of the bonfire, I knew she hadn't grown up with a silver spoon in her mouth like I made it sound. Her mom had a nasty drug habit, and her dad had been nowhere around.

It's what brought her to Haven Brook that night.

I understand her reasons for wanting to escape Cleveland and flee to Philly. We both had set out to start over and break free from the chains that had confined us for so long.

Where I turned to making bets and fighting in the ring to earn money, Austen had gone down this path. She busted her ass to get her internship at the radio station.

She is a fighter, and she was doing what she had to do to chase her dreams.

I may not like it, but I understand it all the same.

"I think we found our guy," Reza said, breaking through my thoughts.

"What'd you find?" I ask, coming up to stand behind him, my eyes scanning over the screen to see what it could be.

"It's a long shot, but this is the best guess I have. The address used to send the email ends with a series of numbers: 101701. At first, I wasn't sure whether it meant anything, but then I noticed one of the usernames was tied to a social media account with the username *jba101701*."

JBA.

JBA. Where had I heard that before?

"Aren't those Justin's initials?" I grit my teeth and turn toward Darren.

Reza does some more typing on his screen before pulling up a picture of Justin. "Is this him?"

Darren's face drops as he huffs out a laugh, and I nod.

"I'll be a sonofabitch," he grunts. "He's a dead man walking now."

"You're fuckin' right he is."

Tension coils in my body and my mind flashes back to the night of the bonfire. He was there. He was right fuckin' there when I made the comment about Austen being fake.

Something about knowing I made that comment and it's him behind this all felt like it was my fault.

I pull the door open to the office, slamming it against the wall as I storm out of the room. Reza shouts at me to chill the fuck out when Darren storms behind me. He pauses, holding his hand up to Reza, telling him he'll take care of it before he chases after me.

I'm unable to control the anger coursing through me. All I know is I need out of here.

I need out of this building.

I need some fresh fuckin' air before I take off and find this fucker, laying my fists into his skull.

"Dude, chill. It's going to be fine. We know who it is now. There's no way he'll live to see tomorrow."

I push through the door, tilting my head toward the sky, and take a deep breath. All this time and it was him.

I stop, folding my hands over my head, pacing back and forth.

I drop them to my side and turn back toward Darren.

"I want him in the ring!" I shout through gritted teeth. "I want him in the ring, and I want to take him for every fucking penny he could get. Do you hear me? You want me back in the ring so fuckin' bad, make it happen."

I push my finger against his chest and Darren holds his hands up in surrender.

"All right. I'll make it happen."

I turn away from him, stalking down the alleyway. He hollers behind me, asking where the hell I'm going.

"I'll walk back to my place. I need a fuckin' minute, man."

I need more than a minute.

I need Justin standing in front of me.

I want to make him pay for what he's done.

# Chapter Sixteen

## RYDER

It takes me an hour before I make it back to my apartment, but it gives me space to cool down.

Austen sent me a few texts before her shift at the radio station. It takes everything in me to keep my mouth shut. She has every right to know it is Justin, but I also have a feeling if I tell her, he won't go through with the fight.

It doesn't make sense to me, though. His dad is loaded. He's set to take over the car dealership his family owns. It's one of the largest ones in the area. What reason does he have to blackmail Austen?

I know there's more to it than what's on the surface. I want to get my hands on him, but I also want the chance to take him for every penny he has.

I slam my apartment door shut behind me, tossing my keys on the counter and kicking off my shoes. I pull out my phone and quickly fire off a text message to Darren.

*Me: Figure out why he'd bother coming after Austen in the first place. Something isn't adding up here.*

He responds back quickly, saying he agrees and he'll do some digging.

My mind keeps drifting back to Austen and the photos I saw on the screen. No matter how hard I try to push the thought out of my mind, I can't tamp the anger from imagining other men looking at them, seeing her the way I do.

I cross the living room into the kitchen, where my laptop is charging on the counter. I hesitate for a brief moment, but when I think back to the sight of her on my bed, spread open in front of me, there's no turning back now.

I unplug the computer and move back into the living room. I open it, setting it on the coffee table in front of my couch.

I quickly type in the web address and search for her username. When I pull up her page, I hover over the subscribe button before reaching into my back pocket to pull out my wallet.

When I'm finally in, I collapse against the back of the couch and scroll through the series of posts on her page. Some of them ranging from photos to various videos, where you can pay a tip to see more content.

I scroll back to the one I saw at Reza's of her wearing a bodysuit with fishnet tights on. Her leg is propped up on her desk chair, showing off her toned legs with her hand covering her pussy, clearly teasing at the fact she had been touching herself.

The thought of her spread open in front of me wearing those tights has me clicking on the video she posted wanting to see more. My breath is caught in my throat waiting while the cursor circles on the screen, loading.

"Jesus fuckin' Christ," I moan, gripping my dick through my pants at the sight of her.

She's lying on her bed, her pants below her knees and her legs are in the air, pressed against her chest. The sight of her fingers dipping into her pussy has me pushing my shorts down to my knees, enough to free my growing erection.

My dick bobs in attention. I cup my balls in my hand, squeezing them gently, attempting to hold off my release. I haven't so much as touched myself yet, but the sight of her is nearly my undoing.

My stomach clenches and my ab muscles flex as I wrap my fist around my dick.

I reach over and hover over another video. I'm like a starved man, eager for more.

It's darker, making it hard to see, but she's dressed in an oversized T-shirt. I immediately start thinking of her wearing one of mine when she stays over. I imagine her walking out of my bedroom in the morning with a sleepy look in her eyes or after a round of fuckin' with a satisfied look glowing on her face.

She takes a seat on a black couch. The video must've been made before she arrived on campus because I don't recognize where she is. She lies back on the couch with her legs spread open. The camera positioned between her legs, pointing at her lower body.

It starts off slow, her fingers running over her legs. Her shirt is covering the parts I want to see. I'm hanging by bated breath for her hands to travel higher.

When her fingers trace under the hem of her shirt, she lets out a soft sigh, and I watch for the telltale sign of her body tremors when it feels good. She releases a low moan.

I'm damn near ready to beg her to pull her shirt up when she starts running her hand over the hem, moving it inch by inch higher up her waist before I get a glimpse of her pussy.

She runs her fingers over the small patch of hair before trailing down to her clit.

I clutch my hand around me, pumping my fist up and down at the sight of her. The slow perusal of her body mixed with the sounds she's making have my body humming with need.

When I finally moved out on my own, I was no stranger to going home with girls. I hung around at parties and was eager to find someone to go home with, not wanting to spend the night alone.

Never, in all of my life, has my body responded the way it does with anyone but her. She's not even here with me and she has me so turned on; I can barely contain the urge to fuck my fist until I come.

I stop, squeezing my hand tighter, holding off my release, not wanting to finish until she's with me.

A few seconds later, she pulls out a small wand and presses a button on the side; the small hum comes to life, vibrating through the screen. She trails it over her skin, up her thigh, toward her pussy. When she gets close, she alternates legs and does the same all over again.

Each pass has her breath hitching. She barely brushes over her clit, releasing a small groan. I'm ready to fall to my knees in front of her and bury my face between her legs, wanting to taste her.

"Fuck," she moans.

The throaty sound of her voice with each heavy breath makes it impossible not to give in, pumping my hand over my dick. When she finally brings the vibrator to her clit, her legs fall to the side, and she pulls her shirt up, her other hand clutching her breast.

"C'mon baby," I moan, urging her on.

It's like she responds to me and says, "It feels so fuckin' good."

I let out a strangled groan, my hand gripping the head of my dick, brushing my thumb over the tip. I rub a bead of precum into my skin, my hips thrusting up, imagining it's her pussy wrapped around me.

Each and every moan she lets out makes it more and more difficult for me to hold back.

Eventually, her other hand finds its way down, her fingers entering her body, one and then two at a time. Her legs begin to tremble and her chest heaves while I match her rhythm. Her fingers glisten, dripping with her arousal.

I tilt my head back and listen to the sounds of her moan, picking up the pace. When she says she's close, I finally roll my head back down to stare at the computer screen and watch her legs quiver, her hand moving back to her breast.

Her fingers brush over her nipple, tweaking the tight bud while she holds the vibrator against her clit.

"Oh fuck."

Her body goes tense before her hips arch off the couch, her release racking through her body. The sight of her coming has me gripping my dick harder, picking up speed until ribbons of cum shoot out.

I rip my shirt over my head, running it over my stomach to clean up the mess I made. The video goes out, and I sag against the couch cushion again. My stomach clenches, my chest heaving as I struggle to catch my breath. Good God, I've never experienced anything quite like that.

My phone vibrates against my foot from where my shorts now sit around my ankles. I find several missed messages from Austen and Darren.

I quickly stand, pulling my shorts up with me before padding down the hall to the bathroom to clean up. When I finish, I scroll through the messages from Austen. She's excited after her boss finally has her starting to help behind the scenes while on the air.

*Me: I just got back to my place now. Proud of you, baby. Come over when you get done and we'll celebrate.*

The bubbles immediately appear on the screen before her message comes through.

*Austen: I should be out of here in an hour. I'm going to make a quick stop by my place, and I'll be over.*

It will be dark by the time she makes the walk over to my place, so I tell her to wait out front of the station and I'll pick her up. I don't want to tell her I'm worried about her walking alone, especially when I know she doesn't suspect Justin is behind the emails.

She responds, telling me she'll see me soon.

I jump over to my messages with Darren.

## *Darren: He's in.*

Darren's been pushing me to come back to the ring. As soon as word gets out, the bets will start pouring in.

I stare back at my reflection in the mirror and the scar lining my browbone. I've been in my share of street fights and fights in the ring, but this is the most important one of them all.

I'm going to make him pay for what he did to Austen.

When I'm done with him, he's going to wish he was a dead man.

# Chapter Seventeen

## AUSTEN

"You're in the mix, with the hottest station in Philly. Rebel 98.1. We have DJ Chris takin' over here at seven o'clock, which means we have time to take one more caller."

Mona grins across the table, holding her hand up to her headphones as she leans in close to the mic.

"We're taking requests right now. Give us a call and you may be on the air with us."

She flips the switch, pulling her headphones off before she collapses back into her chair. She swings her legs around, grinning at me.

I was pumped when I got in today and Adam surprised me with the chance to finally get into the radio booth with Mona. I tried to be patient, knowing it would take time before it would happen. Just having the chance to sit in and be a part of what goes on behind the scenes, seeing all the magic happen, has me amped with adrenaline thinking about the day when it'll be my turn.

"What do ya think? You ready for your turn?" She grins.

"Hell yes." I smile, practically bouncing in my seat.

My head moves in time to the end of Linkin Park's "In the End," mouthing the lyrics. Mona picks up her phone, typing away while we wait for the song to wrap up. I texted Ryder earlier, nearly shouting with excitement over my chance to be here right now.

It feels like one of the first good things to happen to me since moving to Philly. Aside from Ryder.

He takes me by surprise more and more every day. Sometimes I find it hard to believe how easily things have fallen into place with him.

A part of me still feels the need to be guarded, but he continues to be there for me, and it's softening my heart with each day that passes.

Mona sets her phone down, adjusting her headphones, and flips the switch bringing us back on the air.

"Rebel 98.1, you're on the air with us. Tell me what you want, baby."

I grin at her suggestive language. She flashes me a wink, smiling into her microphone.

"Mm, yes." The caller groans into the line, and I bark out a laugh, shaking my head.

I've come to learn since being here, this is part of her appeal. Some of the guys who call in love to be flirtatious toward Mona.

"Well," the groveling voice drags out. "I have a bit of a special request."

"Oh, do tell. Do tell," Mona urges.

"Someone special to me is listening in right now, and I'd like to dedicate this song to her. Can you play "Fake It" by Seether?"

Mona laughs and my face bunches together, confused. Of all the songs to send out to someone, this is the song they choose?

"Violet Grace, baby, this one's for you."

"I can't say I was expecting that," Mona cackles. "You got it! Do you mind sharing your name so she knows?"

"Oh, she knows all right. Don't you, Violet?"

My heart drops at the mention of Violet Grace. Heat radiates over my body. It feels as though my throat is tightening up. The caller knows what they're doing. The urge to run out of here is killing me, but I force my ass in the seat, not wanting to let them intimidate me anymore.

I paste a fake smile on my face, gritting my teeth. I only have a few more minutes left of my shift before Ryder picks me up, and I'll be out of here.

"Your lies won't hide your flaws," the caller adds before disconnecting the line.

Confusion is on Mona's face, but she quickly changes the subject. Her voice is upbeat and happy when she introduces the song before announcing DJ Chris will be taking over next.

Everything after that is a blur. All I remember is Ryder texting me he's outside, and I quickly grab my bag, doing my best to show my thanks to Mona for letting me hang with her before I dart out of there like my ass is on fire.

Ryder is parked in the side parking lot when I dip out through the employee entrance. I make a beeline toward him, pulling the door open and nearly diving in before slamming the door shut.

"What the hell, Austen? Is everything okay?"

His voice is hurried, laced with panic. He sits up, looking through the rearview mirror and around the outside as if suspecting someone's following me.

"Can you just drive, please? I want to get out of here."

As much as I told myself I wasn't going to let this get to me, I can't lie and say it hasn't. The constant fear of not knowing who's behind the messages has me on edge.

Ryder puts the car in drive and bolts out of the parking lot.

We are driving for a few minutes, nearly halfway to his place, when he finally breaks the silence.

"You mind telling me what the hell happened back there?"

"He called me," I mutter, running my fingers through my hair, staring out the window.

"What?" His voice drops low. "Who called you? When?"

"When I was back at the radio station. They called in when we were on air taking requests." I tell him about the song choice and how they dedicated it to me.

Ryder's demeanor turns dark, and the tension rolling off him is palpable. He grips the steering wheel until his knuckles turn white. I slide across the seat toward him, needing to feel closer to him right now.

I press my thigh against his and lean my head on his shoulder while he drives. I notice his grip relaxes before he moves his hand to rest on my thigh.

"Thank you for picking me up," I whisper when we pull into the parking lot to his apartment building.

He parks his car and turns the key in the ignition before dropping the keys in his lap. I reach my hand for his, tangling our fingers together. He rubs his thumb along the back of my hand before making his way up my forearm, brushing over my tattoo.

He seems lost in thought, and I don't blame him. My mind is a mixture of questions and fears spinning like a tornado. Yet, somehow, being next to him helps ease my anxiety the longer we're together.

"I can't take this anymore," I murmur. "I wish they'd go away and leave me alone."

"Hey," he turns in his seat, tilting my head up to look at him, "I'm not going to let anything happen to you. You hear me? This is probably some cocksucker behind a keyboard. I'd never let anyone hurt you."

I nod, leaning my head against his chest. He wraps his arm around me, holding me against him.

"How'd your boss take it?"

It was as if a ball of cotton was stuck in my throat. How do I tell him about the subtle hint to Violet Grace?

I can't exactly tell him without letting him know about my website. A part of me is scared to face what he'll say; I fear he'll somehow look at me differently than he does today.

"Umm, well ..." I exhale harshly, moving to sit up.

I give myself a second to collect my thoughts, staring around the parking lot. I guess it's best we do this here because if he flips out, I can at least tell him to take me back to my dorm.

The dread in my stomach twists like a knife, and I want to crawl into a hole.

"Austen ..."

"So, I have something I need to tell you ..."

A look passes over his eyes I can't quite make out, which doesn't help me with what I'm about to say, but I push the fear aside and go with it.

I move my body to face forward, giving Ryder space. I'm gearing up for the moment he'll want distance from me, so I give it to him first, not wanting the rejection to smack me in the face.

"When I found out I got my acceptance letter, I knew I was going to have to figure out a job. The problem was between school and my internship, I didn't know how I'd balance them all while also making enough money to survive."

He doesn't move, doesn't say anything. I release a heavy sigh and push myself to continue.

"I saw so many people on TikTok talking about their accounting jobs." I exhale a chuckle. "It's not truly an accounting job, you know. They're talking about their secret jobs."

"What do you mean?" His voice is monotone, devoid of any emotion.

"It's basically code for their OnlyFun site."

I let that sentence linger in the air, waiting for any sort of reaction to come, but instead, I'm met with silence.

"Basically, I have a website through OnlyFun where I sell exclusive content to subscribers."

"What sort of exclusive content?"

I know he's not stupid. With social media these days, the word has spread like wildfire. People everywhere have jumped on board with selling their explicit content.

"The photos. The ones they are using to blackmail me. They got them from my OnlyFun site."

He exhales a heavy breath, his nostrils flaring. I lean forward, trying to get him to look me in the eye, but he keeps his gaze forward. Even though we are sitting close together, I can feel the distance between us.

"It's only a job for me. I need the money."

"I know," he says. "Doesn't mean I like it, though."

I reach my hand out toward him again. I expect him to pull away from me, but he takes me by surprise when he slips his fingers in mine.

"You know, if you took this money from your dad, you'd be able to quit."

He was right. How do I explain to him that although Lillian encouraged me to take the inheritance, something about accepting it still got to me? He took advantage of my mom all my life, using his money anytime he was faced with the consequences of his actions.

From the outside looking in, taking his money would solve many of my problems and give him a proverbial "fuck you." Except, something about taking it, after all the bullshit he's put me through, feels as though I'm letting him manipulate me the way he did my mom.

"You still don't know if you're going to take the money, do you?"

"I don't want to talk about it right now."

He shakes his head before his eyes finally find mine. "Fine," he sighs. "I don't like the idea of anyone else seeing pictures or videos of you ... like that. If I had it my way, those would be kept for my eyes only."

I drag my teeth over my lower lip, waiting for him to continue.

"Not only is this putting your scholarship at risk, but you could also take care of your tuition without having to worry. You could focus on school and your internship, get yourself a car, and whatever else you may need while you save up. This could give you a life we never had growing up. I know you don't like your father. Shit, if I'm honest, I'd probably feel the same way you do. Still though, don't you think you sacrificed enough already?"

"If I tell you I'll think about it, will that make you feel better?"

He curls the edge of his lip up and shakes his head. "I'll take what I can get, I guess."

I smile back at him.

"Will you do something for me, though?" he asks.

"What?"

"Darren has a friend who's trying to track down who sent the email by their IP address. Until then, will you stay here with me?"

I stare out at the white apartment building through the windshield. Ryder's apartment windows are open, and the wind blowing outside is causing the blinds to flutter when each gust whips through.

"Okay," I agree.

He flashes me a small smile and tilts his head to the side. "Okay?"

Did he think I was going to put up a fight? The thought of going to sleep every night with

Ryder's arms around me sounds like heaven. Not to mention, I hate being alone in my dorm, knowing Aimee was likely going to be staying with Darren anyway.

"It looks like you're stuck with me now, Irish." I grin.

# Chapter Eighteen

## AUSTEN

"Where the hell are you taking me?" I grumble.

Aimee links our arms together, feeding me with the same line she has since we left our dorm, "I'll tell you when we get there."

The smell of mildew permeates the air. Laser beam lights flicker overhead as we take the stairs down into the old, abandoned train station. A neon sign, which reads "The Devil's Lair," hangs on the wall, leading the way. Something about this feels all wrong.

I had been sitting in my dorm, studying with Aimee, when a text came through that had her sitting up ramrod straight on her bed. Without explanation, she forced me with her, only telling me to grab a jacket and to wear my worn Converses.

I'm questioning where the hell she's taking me the farther we go. The only reassurance I have is knowing we aren't alone. People are huddled in the distance, nearly packed wall to wall, with the sound of heavy bass music beating.

"You'll see soon, I promise. Just come with me!" Aimee shouts.

The stairs lead into the underground tunnels below the train station. The crunch of rocks and gravel sounds beneath my feet. The ceilings are higher in the lower level, with an array of red, blue, and purple lights shooting in all directions.

As we continue into the tunnels, the space begins to open; a large metal cage becomes visible in the distance.

"What sort of kinky shit is this?" I question. My brows furrow in confusion.

Aimee shakes her head, throwing it back in laughter, and moves her hand down to grab mine. She continues to pull me deeper into the crowd, weaving in and out until we get close to the front.

A large rope surrounds the cage to keep the crowd back. In the corner, I notice Darren standing with a group of men, some of them dressed in suits. A briefcase sits near Darren's feet. My mind reels with thoughts of how out of place they look here.

He's deep in conversation with one of the men, a scowl marking his features. He's wearing a fitted black suit matching his dark features. His hair is nearly jet black, styled slicked back. I'm beginning to wonder what business they have with him and here of all places.

Darren reaches his hand out and shakes the man's before being handed a large wad of cash. The man says something to him, flicking his finger in his face, before stepping away. I have no idea what was said but judging by the way Darren's jaw clenches and his nod, I suspect it was met with a warning.

Darren fists the thick stack of cash, handing it to one of the guys next to him, who bends down and stuffs it into the briefcase. Darren turns his attention back on the crowd, and when he does, his gaze falls on mine. His eyes narrow when he finds me watching whatever went down. He folds his arms over his chest and glares at me. The urge to roll my eyes and flip him off burns through me. I've never been a fan of Darren's since the first time we met. Something about witnessing his scheming ways only solidifies that feeling.

Someone taps him on the shoulder, breaking our eye contact, and hands him a microphone. My eyes dart around the room, searching for a sign of what's to come. I wish I knew where Ryder was, knowing if Aimee pulled me along here with Darren, he won't be far behind.

Darren moves to the center of the cage, holding the microphone to his mouth. Before he has a chance to say anything, someone in the crowd shouts, "Let's get on with the blood bath."

A sinister smile spreads across his face, and I tug on Aimee's arm.

"Oh, I fully intend to, my friend. Hold on tight." Darren mocks.

"What the hell is this?" I pull Aimee close to me, shouting in her ear.

"The Ring," she follows up. "Don't be mad at me, but Ryder told me to make sure you were here."

"What the hell did he do?"

Unease causes my stomach to flip, waiting for her response. Instead, she pastes a smile on her face and turns her attention back to Darren.

I fidget, my hands feeling clammy as I tighten them into fists. Something is about to go down, and I don't feel good about it.

"Welcome back to The Ring," Darren's deep voice echoes around us, and the crowd rumbles. "Tonight, we bring you one hell of a good show. Are you fuckin' ready?"

Aimee's bouncing on her feet next to me, cupping her mouth as she cheers along with the crowd.

"Our first fighter comes as no stranger to The Ring. He's one of Eastwood and Kappa Sig's finest, Justinnnn Asterrrr."

The mob erupts, and my jaw goes slack. The crowd parts as Justin walks toward the cage. He is dressed in a pair of red shorts. His chest and forehead are slick with sweat.

The door to the cage flings open, slamming against the side of the ring. He jogs inside before it's shut behind him. He bounces on his feet, rocking his neck from side to side.

As soon as he enters the ring, I know without introduction who he's facing. My nails dig into my palms with the anticipation of his name being announced.

"His opponent is one of the most lethal fighters I've seen hit this ring. He has an iron fist and venom laced in his blood. Get ready for the Wiiiiiiilllldddd Irishhhhhh!" Darren's voice turns into a deep growl, the sound sending a jolt of adrenaline racing through me.

If I thought the crowd went crazy before, the roars that ensue are no match for when Ryder makes his way toward the ring.

His eyes are dark, and his face is hard as if sculpted from stone. I've seen this side of Ryder before, but it's been years. I'm almost fearful of what damage he could end up doing to Justin. The door pushes open, and he strolls into the cage. The crowd explodes when he goes on the attack, heading right toward Justin. He steps toe to toe with him, gritting his teeth, shouting something at him before a devious smile stretches across his face.

"What the hell is going on?" I yell.

"He made me promise not to tell you until after the fight was over."

"Tell me what? What the fuck is there to tell, Aimee?"

Our conversation is interrupted when the sound of the bullhorn goes off, signaling the start of the fight. My eyes dart back to the ring.

Justin moves into a defensive stance, rolling his shoulders, circling the cage. Whereas Ryder is calm and calculated, like a rattlesnake waiting for the right moment to strike.

Justin launches a punch at Ryder, and he dodges his fist, flashing him a wide smile. I shake my head, clenching my jaw with the tension coiling in my body.

I know what he is doing, and he does too. His reaction only seems to dig deeper under Justin's skin. He clenches his jaw, shaking his arms out before coming at him again. When he goes in for a second punch, he's not ready when Ryder sidesteps him again, only this time follows it up with a hook landing it right to his ribs.

Justin clutches his arm at his side, wincing in pain. He tries to shake himself out of it again, but I can see the pain-stricken look on his face.

Ryder, on the other hand, is relishing in it. He uses it as an opportunity to go in for the kill, striking him again, only this time right in the gut with a powerful uppercut. His body folds at the waist right as Ryder rams his knee into his face, sending blood spurting from his nose. Ryder pulls back and lands another blow.

Justin falls to his knees, blood pouring down his face and onto the concrete floor. Darren blows the bullhorn again, calling the end of the fight, before he enters the ring, raising Ryder's hand in the air.

Darren doesn't even give Justin a chance to collect himself or even attempt to stand. Instead, Justin collapses against the pavement, rolling onto his back.

Ryder pushes past Darren, not giving a shit about winning the fight. He falls to his knees near Justin, getting his face low near his. You can see the anger rolling off him as he shouts at Justin, spit spraying from his mouth as his lip curls.

I can barely focus on the sight in front of me. The crowd's screams grow deafening and, for a second, it's as if the room is silent, turning to white noise around me.

I don't even realize it, my legs and feet moving on their own accord, pushing past the rope until I feel the cool metal of the cage against my skin.

Darren says something to Ryder, and it's like a switch flips, his gaze turning over to me. Blood covers his chest, hands, and legs. He moves to stand, stalking toward me.

Any anger he had on his face before is gone. Aimee reaches her hand out, gripping my forearm, shouting at me over the crowd for leaving her.

I don't pay her any mind. The rest of the room fades away, leaving only the two of us.

"I'm okay," he shouts.

"The crowd starts to chant, *"Wi-ld! I-rish! W-ild! I-rish!"*

"Stay with Aimee, you hear me?"

I narrow my eyes at him, and he follows it up with, "I mean it. Please. Stay with her."

I nod, and he turns away, stalking out of the ring, disappearing to wherever he was before the fight began. I take in the sight of the raven spanning his back.

The wings are frayed, battered, and damaged. Yet, like the man beneath it, he's still fighting.

"Why didn't you tell me we were coming here?" I holler at Aimee.

"There's more to it than you know, and Ryder was afraid if you knew the details, you wouldn't show."

My face falls, and I know Aimee sees the change in my demeanor when it does.

"It's Justin," she follows it up. "He is the one who has been blackmailing you. He is the one behind the emails."

The news hits me like a ton of bricks, leaving only the questions swirling in my mind in its wake.

The first one is why, followed by how the hell did he even know about my website. It makes no sense when we met the night of the Kappa Sig party before I ever knew about my dad passing away or the inheritance.

The only explanation I have is the comment Ryder made to Justin the night of the bonfire. When he knew I wasn't interested, when he started to realize there was more with Ryder, he didn't care anymore about hurting me.

Any plan he had to get close to me before must've went out the window, resorting to blackmail. My gaze falls back on the ring as two men help Justin to his feet. He holds a handkerchief to his nose and already has two black eyes forming beneath his bloodshot eyes.

The only thing I can't figure out is how he knew about Violet Grace. No one knew until after the emails started coming out.

My mind shuffles through all the pictures and videos I posted online, from my tattoo to any possible signs as to who I was or where I went to school.

I push past Aimee, not wanting to be here in this dingy tunnel for another second.

"Where are you going?" Aimee shouts from behind me.

"Out of here. You're welcome to come with me, or you're welcome to stay. Either way, I'm done."

# Chapter Nineteen

## RYDER

"How's it feel to be back in the ring?" Darren grins, smacking my chest.

I pick up my T-shirt, using it to wipe the sweat dripping down my face and chest.

"I told you, man. I was only doing this for one reason and one reason only. Don't come asking me to do this shit anymore. I'm done."

His face falls, and he shakes his head. "Do you realize the money you're leaving on the table?"

"Dude, I grew up sleeping on the floor and ate stale food for weeks because my mom couldn't be bothered to go to the store. You think I give a shit about money? I don't want my life spiraling down the same path my mom's did, so drop it."

He holds his hands up and takes a step back.

"I was talking to Reyes before the fight, and he told me he heard Justin was looking for someone to fix his car on the down-low. He was looking to pay them under the table but needed the money from tonight to foot the bill."

My brows dart up. "He has to be up to something if he wants it off the books."

He's right. He has the money and the resources, so why is he going to someone else to help get the work done?

"His money source is gone. There's no tellin' what he'll do now." I am willing to bet he'd take desperate measures, considering he was blackmailing a woman for money.

He's scraping the bottom of the barrel now.

I get dressed and slip out the back of the building toward my car, scrolling through my messages I sent to Austen.

All the adrenaline that had been pumping through me sent me spiraling like a hurricane, and the end was the crash.

Austen is nowhere to be found.

> *Me: Where are you?*
> *Me: Are you still at The Lair?*
> *Me: Austen ...*
> *Me: What the fuck?! What is going on?*

I pull up outside her dorm room. The light to the window above her bed is off. Either she isn't home, or she is asleep. It's after one in the morning, and there's no way I'll be able to sleep until she talks to me.

Even if she doesn't want to see me tonight, I can't go back to my apartment without her. I don't want to be alone until I know what's going on.

I'll sleep in my car tonight if I have to, but I am not going back there without her.

I run my hands over my scalp, dragging them down my face. I massage my eyes and tilt my head back against the headrest. My body aches are creeping in now; I'm feeling tired and worn down. My knuckles are swollen, the tendons inflamed from not fully healing from the fight.

I don't care, though. I did what I had to do to protect Austen, and I'd do it over and over until my last breath.

I pick up my phone again, scrolling through our messages. Nothing seemed off until the fight. I can't help but fear it is the reason for the distance between us.

I only wish I knew why.

I click on her name, pulling up her contact info. My thumb hovers over the call button, resigning myself to one last attempt. I don't want to make this worse and chase her away, but a niggling thought in the back of my mind tells me to try one more time.

I hit the button and press the phone to my ear. It rings twice before a panicked voice filters through the line.

"Aimee?" I ask, my heart rate amping up. "What's wrong? Is it Austen?"

"She's fine," she rushes out. "She's here, in our dorm. She's sleeping, but I can't get her to wake up."

"What the fuck you mean you can't get her to wake up?"

"She's passed out; she won't wake up. I don't know what's wrong with her, but she's making these noises. Like she's having a bad dream or something. I've tried getting her to wake up, but she won't."

"I'm outside. I'll be right up." I end the call and shove the door open.

It doesn't even dawn on me I need Aimee to meet me at the door when I approach, but I'm saved when two students come walking out, caught off guard when I rush past them.

"I'm sorry," I holler over my shoulder, nearly knocking one of them over. "I need to check on someone."

I'm sure I look like a madman running into the dorms. I don't want them to freak out, but I also don't have the time to stop and explain either.

I take the steps two at a time until I reach the second floor outside of their room. I grip the door frames, dropping my head between my shoulders to catch my breath before I knock lightly. Aimee's expecting me, standing at the door in a tank top and a pair of cotton shorts.

She opens the door; a worried look etches her face. Small twinkle lights hang from the ceiling, which is the only light in the room.

My eyes are on Austen immediately. Her blanket is pulled off her, curled in a ball in the center of her bed. My heart seizes for a moment when I realize she's wearing my T-shirt and no shorts.

Her face is scrunched up as if she's upset before the groaning starts.

"See, that's what I'm talking about. I tried shaking her, thinking she's having a bad dream, but she won't move or wake up."

I step over the clothes and bags on the floor, dropping to my knees near her bed. I move my face close to hers, whispering in her ear.

"Austen." I grip her arm, attempting to subtly shake her. Her lips move like she's trying to speak, but nothing comes out.

"Austen, baby, wake up."

Nothing happens. I continue to try to jostle her, but it doesn't work.

I stand and lift my shirt over my head before kicking my shoes off toward the foot of her bed.

Aimee wraps one arm around her waist; the other is massaging her forehead. The worry on her face is palpable.

"She's going to be pissed at me for letting you in here."

"Well, if that's the case, I'm sure she'll be more pissed at me than she will be with you. I'm the first face she'll see when she wakes up anyway."

Aimee's eyes start searching the room as if looking for the answers of what to do. I take a seat on the edge of the bed next to Austen, not bothering to worry about what's wrong with Aimee. All I want right now is to be close to Austen.

My mind filters back to the first night she stayed at Haven Brook and to the night I fell asleep next to her on the floor. I only intended to check on her, but when I saw how upset she was, the sweat dotting her face, I didn't want to leave her with whatever was weighing on her mind.

I knew the feeling of not wanting to go to sleep alone. Even if we were packed into the rooms like sardines, nothing felt more alone than living there. No one cared about us or how we were doing.

I never realized, even in a crowded room of people, it was possible to still feel so alone.

I lean over to pull the discarded blankets over us. I turn on my side and wrap my arms around her waist, pulling her against me.

Her body is tense, cold from the chilly temperatures. She continues to mumble incoherent words under her breath. It takes a moment before it happens, but when my body molds against hers, eventually, she begins to relax.

I don't hear Aimee leave until the door clicks behind her. If I had to guess, she either went to the bathroom or opted to go stay with Darren. I'm surprised she isn't staying with him tonight anyway, but then again, if she hadn't been here, I would've never known something was wrong with Austen either.

Her fingers glide over my forearm wrapped around her before tensing when she reaches my hands. Her body goes rigid before her eyes shoot over her shoulder, connecting with mine. She pushes off me, moving to sit up.

"What the hell are you doing here, Ryder?"

"What's it look like I'm doing?" I squint my eyes in confusion.

She rubs her hands over her face, moving up to grip her hair. She pulls her legs up, pressing them against her chest, closing herself off to me.

"What's going on? Everything was fine between us before the fight; now you're acting like something is up. Why won't you talk to me?"

She drops her hands, staring down at me as if she can't believe I'm asking this question.

"What?" I ask, holding my hands up.

If she knows I subscribed to her OnlyFun account, she isn't saying it. As long as she continues to act like this, I'm going to play clueless.

"I don't want to talk about this right now." She sighs, collapsing back against the bed. She adjusts her pillow, moving far enough away to leave space separating us.

Ignoring her attempts for space, I reach my arm around her body and pull her close to me until her back is once again pressed against my chest. She attempts to wiggle out of my arms, but it's futile. I change the subject entirely. "Were you having a bad dream?"

She stops fighting me, her body relaxing and her arm moving under her pillow. She arches her back, forcing her ass against my dick. I bite my lip, attempting to hold my shit together.

If she's still trying to keep up this whole ploy of being mad and wanting space, she's doing a shitty ass job of it.

She remains quiet, so I continue to press her. "Aimee was here. She was worried about you. You were mumbling and groaning in your sleep, but every time she tried waking you, nothing would happen."

She rolls onto her back, staring up at the ceiling before turning her head to look at me.

"I've been having these dreams. Except it's not a dream, it's real. Ever since the night of my mom's arrest, I've been having them. I was woken up from my sleep when the police busted into our house. That's when I ended up at Haven Brook."

"In the dreams, it's like I'm lying in bed and replaying the entire scene of the cops showing up and taking my mom to jail and me away. My eyes are open, I'm looking around, but it's as if my arms and legs weigh a thousand pounds. No matter how hard I try to fight it, I can't pull myself out of the nightmare. It's like I'm forced to re-live it over and over again."

I grip her chin in my hand, tilting her head up to look at me.

"I'm sorry you have to keep going through that," I say, wanting her to know I mean it. "It seems to happen when I'm stressed or not sleeping well, so I'm not surprised it started up again."

Her eyes meet mine and I want so badly to kiss her right now, but I also don't want to ruin the moment and make this about sex. I can tell this is bothering her. I want her to know I'm here for her in every way she'll let me be.

"How long is she in prison for?"

"Five years."

"Damn." I wince.

"She should only have another year or so unless the judge decides to let her out early on good behavior."

Her tone shifts. Hopefulness exists in her voice. I can't imagine what it must feel like to still have a parent around who gives a shit. It's not that her mom didn't love her or want to be with her, she just lost herself along the way.

"She'd be proud of you and where you are now. You know that?"

She nods, turning on her side to face me. "I know she is."

She lets out a heavy exhale and closes her eyes. I brush my thumb along her cheek before her eyes slowly open again.

I tilt her chin up to me, brushing my lips over hers. She grips the side of my face, pulling me with her as she rolls onto her back. I follow along, moving between her legs.

I rest my upper body on my forearms, leaning in to kiss her again. This time it turns heated when she wraps her legs around my waist, pulling me against her.

She tilts her head back and whispers, "I don't want to think about anything else but you and me." Her hands grip my face, her lips crashing into mine. She opens her mouth, her tongue skating along my lower lip, and I release a low growl.

I pull back from her, jumping over her legs, dropping my sweats onto the floor.

Her tongue darts out, running along her lower lip. Her eyes shoot up to mine, sparkling beneath the dim lights.

She sits up and slips my shirt over her head, dropping it onto the floor next to my clothes. She's not wearing a bra. The sight of her soft nipples has my mouth watering, wanting to taste them.

She lifts her hips in the air, pushing her panties down her legs before toeing them off as well.

I wrap my hand around my dick, pumping it. It dawns on me that any second Aimee could bound through the door like she has before, ruining the moment, but I don't give a fuck.

Her eyes drag over my body, watching me fist my length in my hand.

"Ryder," she moans, tracing a path over her hip up her stomach between her tits. She brushes her finger around her nipple, letting out a soft whimper. "I want you to fuck every thought right out of my mind."

I climb onto the bed between her legs and move in for those pert nipples. I'm nearly salivating at the thought of tasting her, and I don't want to waste another second.

She thrusts her hips up, gliding her wet pussy over my dick. I pull back enough to give her room as she slips her hands between us, guiding me to her opening.

My eyes practically roll back in my head when I enter her, my hips pistoning like a rocket blasting off. Her fingers dig into my back, her legs and pussy tightening around me.

I reach my hands up, gripping her wrists in my hand, pushing them back against the bed. I stare down between us to where our bodies meet, watching as I pull out before pushing back into her.

The sight of her wetness glistening on my dick has me nearly coming apart.

We don't last long. Even with her hands pinned to the mattress, she seeks out her release by lifting her hips off the bed, matching me thrust for thrust until we're both struggling to catch our breath.

I release her hands, moving to change our position. I can tell I hit the right spot when her back arches off the bed, her hand flying down between her legs.

"I'm so close. Oh God, Ryder, I'm so fuckin' close."

Her movements turn jerky, and my hips pick up the pace until we both crash over the edge, riding the high of our release. I tilt my head toward the ceiling, letting out a throaty groan before collapsing against her.

She wraps her arms around me, neither of us moving to separate from the other. In fact, her legs tighten around me, and her nails slowly trace circles into my back, relaxing me further.

It's as though all my energy has been forced right out of me.

A thought hangs on the tip of my tongue. The sudden urge to tell her how I feel sends my eyes shooting open, a spike of adrenaline burning through me.

No matter how close I get to Austen, a niggling fear still exists in the back of my mind. What if she rejects me and pushes me away?

The thought of losing her, along with everyone else I've ever let get close to me, forces those feelings back into the cage I keep them locked up in.

I'll break myself before I let anyone else break me.

# Chapter Twenty

## AUSTEN

I tend to avoid any and all situations that involve talking about feelings.

It's what I'm doing. I'm avoiding Ryder.

Not only because I'm starting to realize the feelings I have for him have grown beyond something fun, but because I know he has the potential of breaking my heart in the process.

The old me wouldn't believe I'd ever trust Ryder O'Rourke with my heart. Yet somehow, the more time we spend together, the more I start to see the man he's kept hidden from the rest of the world.

He showed up at my apartment a few days ago. I knew I was avoiding talking to him and turned to sex to cover up all the feelings I have.

When Aimee told me Justin had been behind the blackmailing and Ryder set up the fight to take him down, I honestly didn't know how to feel.

It made sense why Ryder would be out for venom.

It creeped me out to think about how Justin figured out I am Violet Grace. I still fear what else he is capable of, especially if he's willing to go this far already.

On top of it all, I keep thinking how all of this may have never happened if it hadn't been for Ryder mentioning my dad was loaded at the bonfire.

I push the door open to The Grind, stopping by for some coffee after class. I have the rest of the day free. I told myself I was going to the library to try and study, hoping to avoid the lure of hanging out here for too long, knowing it was inevitable Ryder would eventually show up.

Although, if I am being honest, a small part of me hopes he does.

As if on cue, I spot his car pull along the side of the street outside of the coffee shop. He leans over to roll down the window. The car is one of the old classics where you still have to crank the lever to get them to roll down.

"Hop in," he shouts at me. A group of girls stops, peering into the car before realizing he isn't talking to them. I press my lips together, covering up my laugh at their obvious disappointment.

He shakes his head, flashing me his sexy grin. "Get your ass in here. Let's go somewhere."

The sidewalk is bustling with people. I dart across through a small gap, leaning over to peer my head into the passenger side window.

"What makes you think I'd want to go anywhere with you?"

I'm being playful, but a hint of seriousness coats my voice.

He chuckles, picking up on it. He rubs his hand over his jaw. I notice the five o'clock shadow growing in. The sight of his facial hair makes it even more tempting.

Who am I kidding, though? I'm going to climb in with him anyway.

I'll just put him through hell first.

"I deserve that, I deserve that." He nods before turning back to me. His face turns serious when his gaze meets mine. "I guess I was hoping you'd come because you want to be with me."

My eyes search his face, looking for any sign he could be lying or joking. Anything that would clue me in to the fact maybe that's not how he really feels.

Even though he's always been hard to read, I come up empty.

I reach for the door handle and climb inside, slamming the door shut behind me. I push my bag into the backseat, deciding I'll focus on studying later. I don't have class tomorrow anyway, so I'll use the time to get caught up before and after my shift at the station.

He reaches for the gear shift near the steering wheel and puts the car in drive. I don't bother to pay attention to where we're going until the roads turn more desolate the farther we drive out of town.

I don't ask at first, but after an hour of driving, I begin to wonder where the hell he's taking me.

"Are you trying to abduct me?" I joke.

He lets out a low chuckle. "Not unless you want me to, baby."

I roll my eyes and shake my head.

"Of course, I'm not abducting you." He laughs. "I do want to show you somewhere, though."

I recline back against the seat, sticking my arm out the window, feeling the wind against my hand. My mind drifts off to when I was younger, riding in the backseat of my mom's old Buick, doing this same thing.

Eventually, we pull off onto some back roads, practically in the middle of nowhere. It's such a stark contrast from living in the city. A peacefulness exists out here, away from the hustle and bustle of campus.

He slows to a stop, pulling along the side of the road into a hidden area overlooking rolling green hills.

"I like to come up here when I need to clear my head."

I unhook my seatbelt, staring into the distance. It's almost hard to believe we were only driving for a short time. It's as if the city is nowhere in sight, and now we're left with nothing but the rural countryside.

"Wow, is this even real?" I ask, pushing the door open. We round the front of his car.

I walk to the edge of the cliff. Ryder leans against the front of his car, crossing his arms over his chest.

I chance a look over my shoulder, staring back at him.

"Can you believe this? The view is stunning."

He nods, not even paying attention to the landscape behind us. "You're right. I've never seen anything so beautiful."

I drag my teeth over my lower lip, turning toward him.

He's dressed in a pair of jeans, a red T-shirt, and black Chuck Taylors. Something about this side of Ryder makes it incredibly hard to be mad at him.

I'm still used to the rugged, asshole exterior he's shown me and the rest of the world for years.

Yet, when he's laid back, showing me his sweet side, I can't help but fall for him, even more, every time we're together.

"Why didn't you tell me you knew it was Justin?"

He winces and lets out a heavy exhale. "I didn't want him to suspect something was up or that I knew. I wanted him in the ring unaware, not knowing what was coming."

I shake my head. I still can't help but believe he did it selfishly to avoid having to face his own guilt over the role he played.

"Listen, it didn't make sense to me why he would do this to you. He was seeing you before he even knew about the money. I never suspected it was him until I ..." he trails off.

I turn back to look at him, wondering why he stops. He claps his hands together, avoiding looking at me.

"Until what?"

"Until I found out about your OnlyFun account. I didn't mean to find out how I did, but if I'm putting this out on the table, I might as well be honest. After that first weekend we spent together trying to keep your mind off things, when I saw the pictures he had of you, I was pissed. I wanted to get to the bottom of who it was. I had Darren hook me up with someone who's good with computers. He got into your email, and that's when I found out."

"You hacked into my email?" My jaw drops. "Are you fuckin' kidding me, Ryder?"

"I needed a way to trace back to who had sent the email."

"Why didn't you tell me?" I spit out.

He rakes his hand over his scalp. He drops his arm to his side, shaking his head.

"Just say it already."

His eyes find mine once again.

"Say it, Ryder. Tell me how you were the one who told him and everyone else at the fucking bonfire about my dad having money. Aimee already told me. You can quit acting like you don't know what I'm talking about now."

His nostrils flare. He pushes off his car, walking away from me. He folds his hands over his head, attempting to control the anger etched on his face.

He paces along the side of the road, and I turn back toward the view, searching for something to say to him but come up empty.

"You're right, all right? I felt fuckin' guilty. You think this hasn't been eatin' me up inside since I found out? You think I don't know how you thought it was me who had something to do with it? Do you honestly believe for a second I'd want to do anything to hurt you?"

"You're the one who said you hated me that night, Ryder. How are you going to sit here and try to tell me you didn't want to hurt me when you've ripped my heart out of my chest before?"

His chest heaves with the force of his breaths. "Don't you fuckin' get it? I love you. All right? I fuckin' love you. Seeing you leave for the bonfire with him when I wanted you to stay with me pissed me off. I had no right to be mad, but I was. Okay? What do you want me to say?"

"Yo-you ..." I sigh. "You love me?"

He stares blankly at me, realizing what he said without thinking.

He sighs, shaking his head before he closes the distance between us. He reaches for my hand, pulling me in, tangling our fingers together.

"Of course, I love you," he whispers, almost as if he's afraid to say the words. "I think a part of me has always been in love with you, ever since we first met."

Tears prick my eyes. I can hardly believe this is the same man I met all those years ago, standing in front of me now telling me he loves me.

"I'm sorry I hurt you," he continues on, "but I won't ever be sorry for doing what I thought was right, at the moment to protect you."

I turn my head away from him, blinking through the tears, attempting to wrangle in my emotions.

"I love you too," I murmur under my breath, turning back toward him.

A slow grin stretches across his face. He releases his hold on my hands, gripping my hips before reaching down to grab me by my thighs, hoisting me up into his arms.

He carries me back toward the car, setting me on top of the hood.

"Say it again." His breath flutters against my lips, waiting for me to repeat the words before he kisses me.

I wrap my arms around his neck, pulling him into me.

"Say it," he urges.

"I love you."

"Mmm," he hums, crashing his lips down on me.

His hands find their way to my ass, clutching it in his hands. He pulls back, pressing his forehead against mine.

"I love you too," he sighs.

He kisses me again. The kiss turns more sensual. Every time I'm near him and things get heated, I find it impossible not to want to take it a step further. We both know if we keep this up, I'm going to end up naked on the hood of his car.

On second thought, why am I worried again?

"I need to tell you something else?" he says when our lips break apart a few minutes later.

My heart clenches in my chest, worry twisting in the pit of my stomach.

"What?"

He pulls back enough to look me in the eye, but he doesn't separate from me. I'm not sure if he's serious or teasing me.

"When I found out about your OnlyFun account, I may have gone back to my place and subscribed to it."

My mouth drops, and my eyes widen.

Oh. My. God.

A sly grin stretches across his face, and I can feel my cheeks flame at the thought of him sitting in his apartment, alone, scrolling through the pictures and videos.

"Did you …" I trail off.

His smile grows, and he nods. "I did."

I smack my hand over my mouth.

"I never came so hard in my life."

I push my hands against his chest, climbing off the car. This time he laughs, teasing me.

"Ryder, I'm going to make you pay for this one."

His face turns serious, and he stalks toward me, lifting me back up into his arms, pressing me against the side of his car.

He attacks my neck, nibbling and biting on my skin until his mouth reaches my ear.

"I'll let you get me back for it, but only if you promise to reserve those videos for me."

I grab his face, bringing his mouth to mine. He grunts when my nails drag over his skin, thrusting his hips against me where he has me pinned in place, unable to move.

"Maybe," I mutter, biting his lip.

"I'll let you get me back for it ..." he sighs, his fingers clenching my hips tighter. "So long as you let me make you mine."

I break the kiss, attempting to catch my breath.

"Wh-what?"

"I want you to be mine."

His eyes burn into me before meeting my gaze once more.

"Say it, Austen."

I don't even know if I can find the words, but the second time he says it, the patience in his voice is gone.

"I'm yours."

# Chapter Twenty-One

## RYDER

"Thanks for hangin' with us. This is Austen and Mona signing off. When we come back, we'll have DJ Chris taking over for the night. Have a good one!"

The radio cuts over and a song by Saving Abel starts playing. Austen has started helping with more of the on-air shows. When she told me they were having her take over with Mona tonight, I promised her I'd be listening in.

She and Mona have an excellent chemistry together. Their playful banter made it entertaining in between the music playing.

Ever since the news broke about Justin being behind the blackmail, I've noticed a change in Austen's demeanor I hadn't seen since she first showed up in Philly.

She seems more relaxed, at ease, which brought back the joking side to our relationship.

I flip off the radio, knowing it won't be too long before she'll be heading over to my place. She texted me before she wrapped up for the night, and it seems like we have fallen back into our routine of her staying with me, despite the fact we hadn't talked about it.

I turn on the TV, landing on the nightly news. I don't pay much attention while I mindlessly scroll through my phone. I've gotten in the habit of turning on the TV, simply wanting some sort of background noise.

Since Austen knew I had subscribed to her website, I've checked in a few times to see if she's been online. I hadn't come outright to say anything about it since, but it's been a week since she's posted anything. A few subscribers have commented asking if everything's all right and wondering when she'll be back.

I'm reading over different comments when I hear Justin's name on the TV and my eyes dart up to the screen.

"After nearly two months, police have made an arrest in the death of twenty-three-year-old James Elliott. Investigators announced Justin Aster has been arrested and charged with homicide by vehicle, reckless driving, and leaving the scene of an accident," the reporter says.

"I'll be goddamned," I mutter to myself, just as my phone vibrates in my hand, flashing Darren's name on the screen.

"Dude, did you hear?" I answer.

"Yeah, I just heard. Can you fuckin' believe it?"

I chuckle. Can I believe it? No, but when it comes to Justin, I'm not willing to put anything past him. It all seems to make sense now.

"I guess the reason why he came after Austen was because he needed the money to cover up his tracks. Some guys I know told me he was trying to fix up the car he was driving, keeping it off the books. If he took it to his dad's dealership or if anyone got wind, it would raise questions. It also meant he was at risk of not being able to take over for his dad when he retires, which we know he didn't want."

"The fucker is going to end up right where he belongs," I grunt.

I'm midsentence when the door to my apartment swings open and Austen walks in. She stops in her tracks, staring at me, her brow raising in question.

I hold my finger up to her, signaling for her to give me a second. Darren lets me know he'll keep me in the loop if he hears any more, but I sigh in relief, knowing Justin has bigger fish to fry now and won't be fucking with Austen anymore.

"What was that about?" she asks, shrugging off her backpack, dropping it to the floor.

She's dressed in a pair of dark denim jeans and an AC/DC T-shirt, with a yellow and black flannel tied around her waist. The temperatures have started to shift cooler, the fall weather sweeping into Philly.

Seeing her dressed down like this is so damn sexy. She doesn't bother to wear makeup or dress up like most girls.

I press my hands to my knees, moving to stand, crossing the distance between us. I lean down and wrap my hands around her waist, gripping her hips while I pull her into my arms.

She relaxes against me. Her smile stretches across her face as she tangles her arms around her neck, brushing her soft lips against mine. It starts out soft and sweet before her fingernails drag over my scalp, sending a chill down my spine.

I groan, opening my mouth to her and swipe my tongue along hers. I lift her into my arms, moving her into the kitchen, and set her against the countertop, stepping between her legs.

She locks her ankles around my waist, holding me against her, and I drag my hands over her hips down to her thighs. She whimpers as my hands explore her body, sighing when I trace my lips down the column of her neck, leaving a trail of kisses over her collarbone.

When I pull back, she turns my face to look at her, pressing her palms against the side of my head.

"If you thought you could kiss me as a way of distracting me, you're onto something, but I'm not going to forget what you said when I walked in either."

I chuckle. "I wasn't trying to distract you."

"Mmhm …" she quirks her brow.

"I was talking to Darren when the news came on. I guess they made an arrest in a hit-and-run investigation. You'll never guess who was behind it."

"Who?"

I tilt my head, not needing to say it. Her mouth drops open, and she slaps her hand over her face. "Are you kidding?"

"Nope. Like I said, the motherfucker will be right where he deserves to be."

She sighs. "Wow. I'm, well, I don't …" She shakes her head, seemingly at a loss for words. "I'm relieved."

I massage my hands over her legs and then to her forearms before lifting her palm to my mouth. I press a kiss there before trailing my lips over to the inside of her wrist.

She smiles a lazy smile before her hand folds against my cheek once again, tilting my mouth up to hers as she leans in for another kiss.

"Speaking of Justin," I say, changing the subject. "I've been meaning to talk to you about something since the fight."

Her eyes turn dark, dragging her teeth over her lower lip before biting it. I reach my hand out, brushing my thumb over her lower lip to stop her.

"You don't need to be worried. It's nothing bad."

She nods but doesn't say anything, waiting for me to continue.

I reach my hands down to unhook her legs from around my waist and cross the kitchen, opening the cupboard door. I pull out the empty box of pasta, turning back to stare at her while passing my hand in front of the box as if I'm Vanna White.

Her brows furrow in confusion when I pop the top and turn it upside down, a wad of cash falling into my hand. Her mouth pops open when she realizes how much money it is.

"Ryder, what the hell are you doing?"

I laugh. "When I found out it was Justin behind those emails, I knew he was hurting for money. In fact, I was counting on it. It meant that the stakes were going to be high, and the more we amped up the fight, the higher the bids started coming in. This is the winnings. It's yours."

"Are you kidding me?"

I shook my head, reaching for the other boxes in the cupboard until I had five stacks of $10,000 sitting on the counter. Her eyes were wide, staring between me over to the money.

"What? Why?"

"I want you to quit your job." I shrug. "I'm like you; I don't give a shit about the money, Austen. I'll live in this fuckin' apartment until the day I die if it means I have you next to me."

I reach for the stack of money and walk back toward her, setting it on the counter next to her legs.

"No amount of money in the world will replace what you mean to me. I want you to be mine, only mine. I don't want to share you with anyone anymore."

"I don't need your money, Ryder," she whispers. I clench my jaw, gearing up for the argument that's about to ensue.

Is she fuckin' kidding me? After everything that went down with Justin, this is what we are back to?

She must sense the anger coiling in me. She reaches her hand out, grabbing my forearm and pulling me between her legs once more.

"I decided to take the money from my dad."

My eyes bulge, surprised. The more time passed, the more I started to believe she would decline her inheritance.

"I've been thinking a lot about the day I went to Cleveland to meet with his lawyer. Lillian, my dad's wife, made a comment while I was there, encouraging me to take the money. Even though I don't want a penny from him, someone else deserves it just as much. My mom has a year left in prison. When she gets out, she's going to have a lot of hard work ahead of her to get back on her feet. I don't want her to return to the same life she had, which landed her behind bars in the first place. I decided I'm going to take the money and help take care of her."

I lean forward and brush a kiss against her soft lips. I press my forehead against hers and say, "I think that sounds like a great idea."

"Mr. Morio also said a portion of the money was set aside to take care of my school. I got the papers in the mail today showing the rest of my tuition has been paid in full."

My brows shoot up in surprise before she holds her hand up. "There's more. I decided to shut down my website. It's going to take some time because I'll have to go through and refund everyone who's paid. It's the right thing to do, but in a couple days, I'll be done. For good."

My lips crush against hers, and I lace my fingers through her hair. I pull on the strands, tilting her head back to deepen the kiss. She reaches out, gripping the front of my shirt in her fist. She lets out a deep moan, vibrating against my lips.

Her legs circle my waist again, and I'm half ready to pull her pants down and fuck her right here on the counter.

When our lips eventually break apart, our foreheads press against each other, and our chests heave in an attempt to control our breathing. I squeeze my eyes shut at the emotions racing through me. The urge to tell her how I feel about her is right there, on the tip of my tongue.

"I love you, Austen."

She pulls back, her face softening with emotion. "I love you," I repeat. "I've tried to understand and wrap my head around how we could go from the way things were when you first got here to where we are now, but I don't want to go back there. All I know is when you're here, when I'm with you, I've never been happier in all of my life."

"I love you too," she murmurs. Her cheeks turn rosy, and I grin at the sight.

"As long as I have you, I'll have everything I'll ever need. You're my home."

Tears fill the brim of her eyes, and she smiles. "I hate to break it to ya, precious. I'm not going anywhere."

"Pain in my fuckin' ass," I grumble under my breath.

This time when I kiss her, it's with every ounce of love and passion in me.

# Epilogue

## AUSTEN

"You have a collect call from an inmate at the Cleveland Correctional Center. To accept this call, press one."

The automated message plays in my ear, and I hit the button before my mom's voice filters through the phone.

"Austy, baby. How are you?" she croons.

Sometimes it feels surreal to hear her voice, but in a good way. Before she was sent to prison, it had been a long time since I heard her sober.

I'm back at my dorm room, picking up a few clothes before I head over to Ryder's for the night. I take a seat on the edge of my bed, folding my arm across my chest, pressing the phone to my ear.

"I'm doing good, really good." I smile.

It's the truth too. My job at the radio station has been going well. I am getting more and more time in the booth. Mona has been showing me the ropes, and I'm learning a lot. School has been going well, and we are nearing the end of the semester. I'm looking forward a much-needed summer break.

Then, there is Ryder.

Once we worked through the blackmail and the secrets we had been keeping from each other, I was surprised by how easy things with him had seemed to be. We put everything out there, on the table, and we were left with no skeletons or hidden secrets in the closet.

"Have you heard any news about when you'll be going before the parole board?"

She's up for parole after this month. Although she had gotten into a bit of trouble when she was first locked up, we're hoping they will release her sooner on good behavior.

Otherwise, she has a year left before she is free, and I can't wait for the day to come.

"That's actually why I was calling you, sweetie. I got to stand before the judge today, and they told me they'll be releasing me early. I have to finish out the next two months, and I should be out in early July."

My heart clenches in my chest and tears prick my eyes. I've been waiting for this day to come. We have written letters to each other over the past few years. Early on, I wasn't ready to talk to her about it, but ever since my father had passed, I felt like it was time for me to put the past behind me.

I know I made my share of questionable decisions. As much as I hated the way things happened, it seemed as though she was trying and putting in the effort to rebuild our relationship.

It's all I could ask for. She is the only parent I have, and I don't want to miss out on the chance for us to be close again.

Tears stream down my face and, although I try to cover it up, I release a low whimper.

"Don't cry, Austy. It's all going to be better now, I promise."

When I called Mr. Morio's office a few months back to talk to him about the inheritance, we had a conversation about how I wanted to help my mom get back on her feet when she was released. He agreed to help me with splitting the payments, and I began to set aside money to help my mom when the day she was free came.

I didn't want to make the same mistake my dad had, throwing money at her, out of fear it could lead her down the wrong path again. Instead, I decided I would set her up with a place and help cover her utilities, giving her enough to start her off on the right foot.

It came with the contingent she was doing the right thing: getting a job, a car, and staying out of trouble.

"I guess it's time for me to start scoping out places for you, so you have a place to come home to."

"You know, you could always transfer schools and stay with me if you want. I wouldn't mind having you at home with me again."

"Actually, there's something I've been meaning to tell you ..."

"Uh oh, you're not pregnant, are you?" she quips.

"Hell no." I laugh. Don't get me wrong, I am not opposed to having children of my own one day, but I'm not quite ready for that step yet. Still, the thought of little Ryders running around puts a smile on my face.

She sighs, seemingly disappointed, and I laugh. "I'm sorry, I'm not pregnant, but I do have a boyfriend."

"Well, that's a good first step, huh?" She chuckles.

"Maybe someday that will be in our future, but right now, I'm focusing on school and my internship. I'm wrapping up here in a couple weeks."

"You got a good head on your shoulders, kid. I can't take credit for how you turned out, but I'm damn proud of you. I hope you know that."

"You did the best you could, Mom."

"I did, but still, I could've done better. I promise you that'll change, though. I can't go back and make up for the past, but I can certainly make sure it doesn't repeat itself again. It will be different this time."

"Good, that's all I want."

We spend the next few minutes talking about Ryder. I tell her how we first met and how we were reunited when I first arrived at Eastwood. I leave out the parts about him being a royal jackass at first, not wanting to sway her opinion of him.

It doesn't matter anymore anyway. The people we are now, especially together, is different than the people we were back then.

She promises to call me next week and to keep me updated on when her release date will be. When the call disconnects, I drop my phone onto the mattress next to me. The weight of the news lifts from my chest, and an overwhelming sense of peace washes over me.

All I want to do, in this moment, is be with Ryder.

I finish shoving my change of clothes and toiletries into my backpack, along with my laptop and books. I don't plan to do any studying tonight, but I also don't have a clue when I'll be back here either. Aimee has been staying with Darren's anyway. Neither of us has any desire to come back here, and the more time I spend with Ryder, the more I understand why she is always away.

My phone vibrates with a text from Ryder telling me he's here. I peek out the window and find him standing outside his car, leaning against the passenger door, staring up at me.

When he sees me looking out onto the terrace, he lifts his hand and gives me a subtle wave. He's wearing a backwards hat and his standard denim jeans with a black T-shirt. It's his staple.

Although he recently added some new graphic shirts to his collection.

He's still waiting for me when I jog down the stairs and out the door. He reaches for the door, opening it for me, and I grin. "Who knew Ryder O'Rourke was such a romantic?"

He rolls his eyes and holds his hand out to me. "Only for you."

I hum, gripping his shirt in my fist, pulling him toward me. He comes easily, leaning down and pressing a kiss to my lips. I know I'm causing trouble when I open my mouth, swiping my tongue along his lower lip, earning me a low growl.

"You're pushing it," he mutters, pulling back.

I shrug, moving to get in, but not before he swats me on my butt.

"Pain in my ass," he follows up before shutting the door behind me.

"What are we going to do tonight?" I ask as he pulls off campus, heading toward his place.

When he asked me on a date tonight, I figured he had something specific planned, but the farther we get from my dorm and closer to his house, I begin to think I misunderstood the plan all along. "I tried coming up with something fun for us to do. I thought you'd like to get out and try something new." I stare out the window.

I love the thought of him putting in the effort to pick something he thinks I'd like.

When we pull into the parking lot of his apartment, I turn toward him. With my brow raised, I ask, "You thought this was something new and fun?"

He laughs and shakes his head, opening the door and climbing out. He doesn't bother answering me and I move to push the door open before he jogs around, helping me out.

I grin up at him, remembering my earlier comment about him laying on the romance. He takes my backpack from me and leads the way into his apartment, holding the door open for me both times.

A makeshift fort is set up with blankets draped all over the living room. I drop my bag near the door, making my way into the room.

I put my hand over my mouth when I see the mattress on the floor with the bed made up. A bowl of popcorn, drinks, and snacks sit in the center. I turn toward Ryder, wanting to tell him how sweet and thoughtful he is, when I notice he's holding the remote in his hand.

"I thought we could start with your favorite. Who doesn't love watching a good murder episode before bed?" he deadpans.

"You sure know how to romance the pants right off me." I chuckle.

He flashes me a wink, kneeling on the floor, pulling the curtain aside, and climbing into the fort. I follow behind him, reclining back against the mountain of pillows pushed up against the front of the couch.

He picks up the remote and clicks play on the Netflix documentary we've been talking about. Ever since I saw the trailer, I've told Ryder how I was looking forward to watching it.

"I talked to my mom before you picked me up."

We hadn't really talked about how things would go between us once the semester wrapped up. I hadn't planned on leaving, but he knows I have to be out of the dorm. He's made comments before about me staying with him for the summer until I went back to school.

With my mom getting out sooner than I thought, that was going to change things.

"Oh yeah? How'd that go?"

"I guess they are releasing her early. The judge signed off on it and everything. She has about two months left, and then she'll be free."

"That's great." Ryder smiles, leaning in to kiss me. I press my palms against the side of his face, soaking in his lips.

"I've been meaning to talk to you about the end of the school year. Now that she's gettin' out and I have the summer open, I thought it would be good for me to head back to Cleveland for a bit. Help her get situated and back on her feet."

He's lying on his side, propped up on his arm. He turns his attention back toward the TV, seemingly lost in thought.

"What does this mean for us then?" he asks, tilting his head up to look at me.

"What do you mean?" My brows furrow and my stomach flips.

This wasn't where I thought this conversation was going to go, tonight of all nights.

"I mean, I know we hadn't talked about it before now, but I guess I was hoping nothing would change between the two of us. Cleveland is only a couple hours away. You're welcome to come stay with me, if you want, or I can make trips back here on the weekends to spend with you. I will only be gone for a couple weeks, and I'll be back for the rest of the summer."

He nods. He turns his focus on the TV again, his eyes losing focus.

I, on the other hand, have pushed away the thought of watching it entirely. I'm more focused on the change in his demeanor, wanting to fix where this is going before things spiral any further.

"Hey," I say, reaching for his arm, pushing him to roll over on his back.

I swing my leg over him, straddling his lap. He's still sitting up, with the mountain of pillows beneath him. I lean my body over him, staring into his eyes.

"What's wrong?"

"Nothin'," he says, but I can tell something's off.

I grip his chin in my hands and lean forward, kissing him again. His hands graze up my thighs, toward my hips, holding me against him. His mouth opens to me, and I swipe my tongue against his. He releases a low moan, vibrating against my mouth, his hips moving up to brush against my center.

I pull back, staring into his eyes, and whisper, "Tell me."

He sighs. "I don't want you to go."

A look passes over his face, but before I can analyze it further, he shakes it off, pushing it away.

"I won't be gone for long. You won't even get a chance to miss me. Like I said, you can come visit me, and I'll make the trip to come see you. It will be a few days in between, max."

"You don't get it," he interrupts. "I hate being here without you."

It's as if he reached into my chest and gripped my heart, squeezing it in his iron fist.

"I've spent most of my life alone, and now that I know what it's like having you around, I don't want to go back to what it was like before this."

I attempt to swallow down the emotions lodged in my throat.

"I've never craved being with someone until I got the taste of being yours."

"I'll still be yours, whether there are a hundred or a thousand miles separating us. I'll always be yours."

He reaches his hand up, slipping his fingers into my hair, and pulls me down until my lips crush against his. I wrap my hand around the front of his throat, feeling his moan rumble against my palm.

Everything about Ryder consumes me. The feelings I have for him, and when I'm with him, could break me if I were to lose him.

"Come with me," I whisper against his mouth. "Please. My mom needs me, but I need you. Come with me."

He hesitates for a moment. I worry he's overthinking it, or maybe he's giving me a chance to take it back, but I don't. It's not going to happen.

"Ryder ..."

"I'll go. If it means being with you, I'll go wherever you want me to."

I exhale a heavy breath in relief, the smile spreading wide across my face.

"I love knowing those words made you smile like this."

I respond with the only thing I can think of saying.

"I love you."

It's his turn to smile, and the sight of his grin fills me with more happiness than I could ever begin to put into words.

"Does this mean I get to call you my boyfriend?"

He laughs. "I mean, if that's what you want to call me, why not?"

My face turns serious, and I narrow my eyes at him. "Well, what the hell would you call me?"

"Mine."

# Bonus Epilogue

Want more Ryder & Austen?

Sign up to receive their Bonus Epilogue at:

www.authorbrookeobrien.com/wildirish

# Books by Brooke

*A Rebels Havoc Series*

Brix
Tysin – Coming Winter 2021

*Men of Blaze*
Personal Foul
Reckless Rebound – Coming to the Cocky Hero
World

*Tattered Heart Duet*

Torn
Tattered

*Hearts Compass Series*

Where I Found You
Lost Before You
Until I Found You
Now That I Found You

*Standalones (In order of publication)*

Wild Irish
Sacrifice
*Sacrifice will be a spin-off in the Salvation Society and A*

WILD IRISH

*Heart's Compass World*

**Learn more and purchase your copy at:**
www.authorbrookeobrien.com/booksbybrooke

# About Brooke

Brooke O'Brien is an author of steamy and swoon-worthy contemporary romances.

She believes a love worth having is worth fighting for, and she brings this into her stories where her characters risk it all for love.

If Brooke's not writing or reading, she's probably spending time with her family, binge-watching the latest crime documentary, indulging in chocolate, or watching Hawkeye football or NBA basketball.

She loves to interact with readers! Keep in touch with Brooke by following her on social media, subscribe to her newsletter, and join her exclusive Reader Group at:

www.authorbrookeobrien.com/follow.

# Acknowledgments

My Boys – I love you more than anything on this earth. Everything I do is for you.

To my AMAZING beta readers – Kristen, Candyce, April, and Ana. Thank you for reading Austen and Ryder's story before anyone else, for your honest feedback, and helping me make their story better. I'm so grateful for you! <3

My Rebels Babes – I love being able to connect with all of you in my Reader Group. I feel like I've found a place where I can share with you my triumphs and crazy ideas, as well as catching up with you about everything going on in our daily lives. I'm so thankful to have all your support.

To the fantastic bloggers and my Rebel Release Team, thank you for being a part of this one. I'm excited to hear what you think of Austen and Ryder. I hope you know how grateful I am for every one of you.

Kim Cermak – Thank you SO much for everything! You help keep me sane so I can try to focus on writing, and I appreciate you so much!

Jen with Wildfire Marketing – Thank you for all your hard work and support in getting this book in the hands of readers. I can't thank you enough for all your help!

Julie and Jacquelyn – I don't know what I'd do without our group chats and your motivation to keep writing. Thank you for your support! It means so much to me.

April – Thank you so much for your friendship. We've grown close over the past year and I'm so thankful to have you in my life, both as a book friend and a real friend.

Kristen – You keep it real with me, always! It's what I love about you. Thanks for riding my ass when I need it, but also reminding me to be patient with myself too. Girl, you're stuck with me now! LOL! Not even sorry about it either.

Candyce – You've helped me in so many ways since we've first met. I'm so appreciative of all you do behind the scenes. Thank you for everything!

Kate Jessop and Lyssa Cole – What would I do without you? I don't want to find out. Thank you for being there for me when I need to brainstorm an idea or tell me it's going to be okay when I need to hear it.

My editor, Amy Briggs. I've enjoyed working with and learning from you! Thank you for all your hard work on this project and helping me learn along the way.

Visit my website at www.authorbrookeobrien.com.

Edited by Amy Briggs, Briggs Consulting Inc.
Proofread by Briggs Consulting Inc.
Cover Design by Tash Drake, Outlined With Love Designs
*Version: BMO09102021*

Made in the USA
Monee, IL
04 November 2021